SHANGHAIED

Books by the Author

LESLIE & BELINDA MYSTERIES
Daredevil
Shanghaied
Rambler
Coming August 2017
The World's Longest Yard Sale - is Murder

Pickett House: Tennesee Haunting Fiction

PARLOR GAME MYSTERIES
Hanging Tobacco

12/12/2022

SHANGHAIED

A LESLIE & BELINDA MYSTERY

by

Linda S. Browning

Buddhapuss Ink ● Edison NJ

Cover Art based on design by Svetlanaprikhnenko, Dreamstime.com
Cover and Book Layout/Design by The Book Team
Editor, MaryChris Bradley
Copyeditor, Andrea H. Curley
ISBN 978-1-941523-13-1(Paperback Original)
First Paperback Edition June 2017

Learn more or contact the author at:

Facebook: LindaSBrowningAuthor
Twitter: @LindaSBrowning
Website: lindabrowning.net

DEDICATION

My LESLIE & BELINDA MYSTERIES will forever be dedicated to my best friend since the summer before we entered the eighth grade. Lynne, these are for you.

Thanks to all the oddball people who have inhabited my life thus far: family, friends, neighbors, enemies, et al. Some are no longer with us, but their eccentricities live on.

Chapter One

shang·hai *transitive verb* \ˈshaŋ-ˌhī, shaŋ-ˈhī \ 1. To put by force or threat of force into or as if into a place of detention. 2. To put by trickery into an undesirable position.

~*Merriam-Webster*

One of the most dangerous pursuits imaginable is tracking a wounded, wild animal, yet that's how I spent my morning. I took my dog, Riff-Raff, along for protection. Riff is a Maltese/some-other-kind-of-small-dog mixture who looks more like an animated dust bunny than a dog.

This morning Riff would not stop yapping at the kitchen window, so I went to investigate. There were two deer just a few feet from my deck munching on some shrubs. I don't get overly excited about munched shrubs, but it surprised me to see deer this close to my townhome. One had a bad front leg, causing the animal to walk like a peg-legged pirate; running would be out of the question for the poor thing. The crippled animal hobbled and nibbled while his/her buddy would bound away, only to return a few minutes later. For twenty minutes, Riff and I watched them until they meandered out of sight.

We have a lot of deer in Fairlawn Glen, or the Glen, as we relocated locals call it. They might be as dumb as sock puppets, but they are beautiful, ballet-like creatures, and I enjoy watching them.

At sixty-eight years of age, I'm in good health despite one creaky, arthritic knee that's more noisy than painful. According to my driver's license, I'm five feet two inches, which I admit is an overstatement. I maintain my 130 pound figure through diet rather than exercise. I avoid all activities that lead to perspiration…my own and others.

The Glen is picturesque, with five golf courses and eleven man-made lakes. There are lots of social clubs promoting all sorts of nonsense, including a racket game known as Pickleball. They even have tournaments for this schizophrenic mishmash-of-all-racket-type-games-ever-invented-by-man all rolled into one. The rules of play are as impossible as they are unintelligible.

• • •

It was getting close to 9:30 A.M., so I was close to getting into the swing of the day. My best friend in the entire world, Belinda, is a morning person. She annoys the hell out of me. Still, when I need help, I usually call her first. It was her idea to call the Safety Department to report the lame-deer sighting. She was an emergency room nurse once upon a time in Philadelphia and believes she is an expert on everything health related. She pooh-poohs my theory that I am allergic to the collective sweat of old people. I'm still doing research.

We are both retired and became widows after moving to the Lake Manchester Townhomes. I don't mean to imply that the townhomes killed our husbands. That was not the case. I live (Tom-less for the last five years) in Unit 2, and Belinda (now two years Frank-less) in Unit 5. My husband of almost forty years dropped dead at the age of seventy-one. He met God when he keeled over from a heart attack mid golf swing.

All I got for my effort was reaching the Safety Department's answering machine, so I decided to check out the status of the wounded deer myself.

Clipping Riff to her retractable leash, we were greeted by my friend hustling down her front walk. "I knew you were going to chase those deer, Leslie; I just knew it. Why aren't you wearing a coat?" Belinda looked as if she was running the Iditarod—definite overkill for early October in Tennessee.

I had on a light jacket. I have a high-core temperature and, therefore, a high metabolism. I don't have to run a 10K race to burn off the calories every time I eat a doughnut.

"This qualifies as a coat. I come to you equipped with sleeves, pockets, and a zipper. Everything one could ask for in a coat."

"You don't even have a hat. You need to take better care of yourself."

"You are only two years older than me; thus you're far too young to be my mother."

She harrumphed and fell in beside me.

"You didn't see the deer?"

"No, obviously I've seen a lot of deer around here, but I haven't seen one who appears to be injured. The poor thing, could you tell whether it was a recent injury?"

"How would I know? You were the nurse. I was a geriatric social worker. If the deer requires counseling or wants me to sign him up for Meals on Wheels, then my skills would be appropriate to the situation."

We walked the length of our complex and peered around the back of Unit 20, scanning the rear of the townhomes and their patios. Nary a deer in sight. Not one on the patios or lingering on the lawn that sweeps in a graceful arc toward the lake.

"They must have gone off into the woods," I theorized.

"Oh, well...mission accomplished, no gimpy deer!" she quipped.

Riff and I set off across the manicured lawn toward the thickly wooded area, and my best friend followed. "The woods are quite lovely this time of the year," I said.

"Yes, quite."

We moved through the leaves, being careful where we stepped.

"Be careful where you step, Belinda." I have a professional inclination to watch out for old people, so I try to be attentive. Such a scintillating conversation.

"Me? You're the one with the bad knees."

"Knee...I have only one bad knee. Just like the poor, little, gimpy deer out here."

"Did you call the Safety Department?" Belinda asked.

"Yes, I called the Safety Department. I got the answering machine. Evidently Chief Cutie-Pie is not manning the phones this morning." We both enjoy ogling Quinn Braddock, the seventy-two-year-old chief of the Department of Public Safety in the Glen. He is a silver-haired eye candy of a lawman.

We were making a racket shuffling through the leaves and surprised a bunch of wild turkeys who appeared from nowhere. They startled me so badly that I danced in place, bobbling Riff like a limp, floppy football. Riff goes tearing after anything that moves like a hyperactive earmuff, so I had tucked her safely in my arms when we entered the woods. The turkeys went running and gobbling off in that jerky, lurching scuttle of theirs—scrawny, funny-looking creatures—more cartoon than fowl.

"Eeek!" Belinda's shriek could break glass, and her scream could double as the siren on a fire truck. This was definitely a shriek.

I've been known to erupt into a fabulously girly scream on particularly horrific occasions. Most of the time I inhale with a loud, gasping, inward snort...not even remotely feminine.

There's not much call for horror in our retirement community. The Glen is usually a safe place to live. Each week I receive an e-mail encapsulation of recent crimes perpetrated on the citizens. Recently somebody stole a clothes dryer. I can just see someone wandering into their laundry room and asking themselves, "What's different about this place? Hmmmmm...there's the washer; there's the sink...hmmmmm.

Something's missing, but what?"

Fairlawn Glen will never make the top ten list of cities with high murder rates. Occasionally something does go horribly wrong here, but when that happens, I tend to notice and get the itch to investigate. Belinda is not overtly curious by nature, but she's always game for an adventure with just the tiniest encouragement on my part.

"I don't see our bum-legged Bambi or his/her buddy anywhere. I say we call off this adventure and go to your house so you can make us some coffee." I was beginning to get chilly...something I would never admit to my know-it-all friend.

"Why do *I* have to make the coffee?"

"Because we both know you make better coffee than I do. Besides, I have to get my acrylic nails done this week. They've gotten so long I can hardly flip the switch on the coffeemaker."

"True. I just don't want to be taken for granted. Those nails of yours are lethal weapons."

"Best friends take best friends for granted and watch out for each other. That's how it's supposed to be. If a maniac attacked you in my presence, I would poke out his eyes with my tenpenny acrylic nails. Now, that's true friendship." We turned around to retrace our steps, but we couldn't find them. "Best Friend, I'm afraid that we are lost. Lost in the vast wilderness of Fairlawn Glen. In two weeks, some poor dog walker will stumble upon our cold, lifeless remains. Just like Roy Conklin's nephew, Eric, unless that poor boy is still picking his way through the Idahoan wilderness."

"Oh, shutup. It isn't funny, you know."

Well, yeah it is, in a warped kind of way. Eric was supposed to be some sort of survivalist, and he went and got himself lost in the Idahoan wilderness. I didn't even know Idaho had a wilderness until Roy's nephew wandered off into it, alone. I looked it up on the Internet.

Sure enough, Idaho has a wilderness. Belinda and her prayer group at the Methodist church still pray weekly for Eric to hack his way free of the potato-vined wilds of Idaho. I don't see it happening. It's been five months and no sign of Mr. Potato Head. I figure he either crossed paths with a mountain lion or a bear, or he disappeared on purpose. Either way, I don't see how I can do anything about it. I didn't tell him to go out there without a cell phone/GPS tracker thingy…alone.

Belinda was looking this way and that through the trees and finally said, "It's this way."

"How do you know? Are you checking for moss on trees or something?"

"No, I can hear the garbage truck. Come on."

Now that she mentioned it, I could hear it too. Kicking my way through the leaves, I wondered aloud, "There aren't any squirrels out here. Don't you find that strange? No chipmunks either. I'll bet the bears scared them all off…or ate them. There aren't any forest critters running around out here."

"What about the wild turkeys? They qualify as forest creatures."

"Wild turkeys would be able to fly away. Those goofy-looking, stork-like things are fast!"

"Turkeys don't fly, Leslie."

"Sure they do. They're birds."

"Chickens are birds too. How many chickens have you seen flitting about from tree to tree? I think the best they can do is flap and hop away."

I yelped as something plunked me on the head, and then on the shoulder, causing me to dance into Belinda. "Yikes, what the heck was that?"

She started laughing, "Ha-ha-ha…you ticked off some squirrels. They're dumping acorns on your head! Ha-ha-ha!"

I stared up into the trees. "Those aren't squirrels up there. See, on that branch over there? It's a wild turkey!"

She continued to laugh. "Is not. Ha-ha-ha!"

I rubbed my head where the acorn had bonked it. "Speaking of bears, I wonder if the bears are all hibernating already?" Earlier this summer we had a scrawny little bear wandering around the Glen, and everybody was on bear watch, especially me. I carried wasp spray everywhere I went.

"There was only one bear around our complex, Leslie, and no one saw it except Evelyn Lancaster in Unit 18, and she isn't a credible witness. Besides, we weren't speaking of bears."

"Mrs. Towers saw the mangled hummingbird feeder with that sweet, syrupy stuff all over Evelyn's patio. She even saw big paw prints smack in the middle of the syrup."

Still carrying Riff, I followed her out of the trees and stepped onto the lawn perimeter of our complex. I set Riff on her feet, and she shook herself to resettle her fur.

"That bear is gone Leslie, and you know it."

"Maybe so, but it wasn't the only bear around these here parts, you know. Dangerous creatures live outside, Belinda. I'm thinking about opening a retirement community down in The Villages where people never have to go outside. I've decided I don't like the outdoors."

"The Villages are in Florida. You hate Florida: alligators and imported boa constrictors and all."

"Sure, but they're outdoors. My idea is a retirement community where everything is connected by acrylic tubes, sort of like hamster tubes. A senior citizen could leave their house and enter the acrylic tube and drive a golf cart or something to the grocery store and back without ever having to go outside. I could market it to agoraphobics. It would be like living inside a force field. Oh, and everything would be reinforced to withstand hurricanes. What do you think? Want to invest?"

"Yeah, I'll get my financial people right on it. Personally, I don't think you spend enough time outdoors. You need to get more oxygen to your brain. Besides, every retirement community needs at least one golf course. How could you have a golf course sealed under an acrylic bubble? Golf balls would be ricocheting everywhere like shrapnel!"

"Hello, Belinda? I believe I referenced agoraphobics. Agoraphobics don't play golf."

We were walking the expanse of tended grass separating the woods from Unit 20, and the start of our landscaped complex. We were heading for the boardwalk that is actually a blacktopped path. We prefer to refer to it as the boardwalk. It borders the shore of the lake in a curving fashion with ten piers jutting into the water like splayed fingers. A line of stationary pontoon boats bobs up and down at their docks. Pontoon boats are big, clumsy-looking things that somehow manage to float.

The townhomes were built in groups of two with one adjoining wall, and the floor plans mirror each other. My mirror image is Unit 1, currently occupied by Ron and Charlene Frey. Ron and Charlene are from New York and spend December through mid-April in Florida… or as Charlene likes to say, they "go south for the winter." My husband and I relocated to Middle Tennessee from Michigan upon retirement. Tennessee is south enough for me.

Ron has an affectation for rocks—that is, moving them around the yard constantly. It isn't as though I spend all my time spying on the neighbors, but one cannot help noticing recurring oddities. My mother had a thing for rocks. She used to drag a rock home for her "rock garden" as a souvenir whenever we went on vacation. Unfortunately, we never went anywhere. Vacations amounted to one week each year. All we did was hang out in Kentucky at one of our respective grandparents' farms. Mom's rock garden amounted to Michigan and Kentucky rocks. She claimed also to have a few from Ohio.

Mrs. Towers, our eighty-five-year-old, widowed neighbor, called to us from her patio. She is *the* primary source of information around here. The poor lady has been using a walker since she broke her hip. She has one of those "Help I've Fallen" gizmos, but it never seems to be anywhere close at hand when she falls and can't get up.

"What were you girls doing in the woods?" Not much gets past her.

We stepped off the boardwalk and crossed the lawn in response to her call. Fortunately, the sprinkler system is pretty much done for the season. The sprinklers are hooked to a pump that shoots out lake water for healthy lawn maintenance. Personally, I believe lake water to be chock-full of bacteria from the unfortunate excrement of lake-dwelling life. I'm not all that crazy about that nasty water drenching my immediate landscape. Since there isn't much I can do about it, I try to remain alert for newly sprinkled grass. Riff doesn't like to walk on grass in general except to go potty. Even then, she does so grudgingly.

I unclipped Riff's leash, and she flew to Mrs. Towers.

"Hi, Riff, you little devil you. Come on in, girls, and tell me what you were up to in the woods." She thumped her walker up and around, stumping her way through her patio doorway, and took a seat at her kitchen table without waiting for our response. We followed her inside. Riff was sitting on Mrs. Towers' foot, gazing up at her with adoration. I one-handed the mutt and plopped her in my friend's lap.

"Thank you, Leslie." Mrs. Towers nuzzled Riff happily.

Taking a seat, Belinda said, "Leslie saw a gimpy deer nibbling on her bushes and was worried, about the deer that is, not the bushes. We couldn't find it though."

"She's okay. I'm surprised she was down as far as your unit, Leslie."

I sat with an *oomph*. "She? How do you know the deer is female?"

She chuckled at my naïveté. "Because Jane Doe has lady parts, of course."

"You looked?" I don't know why I was surprised, but I was.

"Sure, I checked her over when she first started showed up. Jane and her companion, that is. They've been hanging around our area for about six weeks."

I laughed. "*Jane Doe!* That's rich, Mrs. Towers."

Grinning, she stroked Riff's fur. "*I* thought it was clever."

Leaning into the conversation, Belinda asked, "Was Bum-Leg, um…I mean Jane Doe, already injured when you first saw her?"

"Yes. I've no idea what happened to the poor thing, but she doesn't appear to be in any pain. I know for sure that her appetite isn't impaired; she doesn't appear to be underweight." She allowed her voice to trail off as she suddenly became fascinated by something on Riff's collar.

I pointed at her with great glee. "*AHA!* You've been feeding Jane Doe, haven't you? I'm surprised at you. Aren't you the one who told everybody not to leave birdseed and stuff out as it attracts bears?"

"Bears, Leslie. I never warned anyone about any man-eating deer. Besides, I don't feed Jane, really. Once in a while I may toss out part of a head of lettuce or something. You know how you can never finish a head of lettuce when you live by yourself?"

That's true. Lettuce gets all slimy when you aren't looking. "We won't turn you in to the wildlife authorities. How in the world did you get close enough to Jane to check her out?"

"Jane is very docile. It didn't take much encouragement on my part to befriend her. Her companion is still skittish, but Jane would come in the house if I let her."

We chatted about this and that until I brought up the subject of Pretty Polly. "I'm beginning to wonder if my unit is haunted."

"Oh, Leslie, get serious." Belinda laughed. "Tom is not haunting your townhome."

"Oh, not Tom…no, if Tom were unable to sever his earthly ties, you'd find him on the golf course working on his putt…or slice…or whatever. He isn't the one hanging around the house."

"Speaking of Tom, you know, dear, you really need to do something with his ashes," Mrs. Towers clucked. "Keeping the man in your clothes closet like that is not very respectful. I might haunt you too if you did that to me."

"Tom is in a very respectful, tasteful box. I will do something with him just as soon as I decide what. Anyway, Tom is not the ghost."

"Leslie, why are you imagining ghosts? You're getting bored again, aren't you? You always come up with off-the-wall stuff when you get bored. There is a new play down at the Clifton Showhouse. Somebody related to a famous country star is supposed to be in it: Loretta Lynn, or Dolly Parton, or somebody. I'll go with you. It will be good for you to get out with people and listen to some good music."

"One cannot assume that fabulous talent is passed along to family relations. Maybe Barbra Streisand was the first one on both sides of her family who could even carry a tune. According to my mother, her uncle Kenneth was popular at the county fair juggling gourds, but I can't pour a glass of milk without spilling it. Besides, the last show I let you talk me into was that singing thing about the French war." We went to see *Les Misérables*. A bunch of actors lurched and lunged around the stage warbling sort-of-like-talking songs. It was torture, *truly* miserable. "I'm out with people right now. You and Mrs. Towers qualify as people. Seriously, Perfect Polly keeps going off all by herself! I'll be way in another room, and she starts to chitter up a storm!"

I bought Perfect Polly at the Dollar General Store for $4.99. She is a lifelike, green, plastic parakeet that tweets and turns her head whenever she detects motion. I bought one for Belinda too, but her cat tore Polly's head off after the first five tweets.

"Riff is probably setting her off."

"Nope, every time Polly has gone off, Riff is sitting with me on the sofa. I tell you, it's downright eerie."

"So, turn the stupid parakeet off...or take out the batteries."

"That isn't any way to solve a perfectly good mystery."

"The Perfect Polly mystery!" Mrs. Towers cackled at her witticism. "I've seen the commercials on TV. It's activated by motion or changes in the light. Maybe it's light shining in a window, slight vibrations, stuff like that, a bird flying by the window maybe. I doubt that plastic parakeet was designed at the Massachusetts Institute of Technology, Leslie, but it isn't going off for no reason...well, unless she is related to my dear, departed husband, Arnie. It never took much to set that man off. Did you buy Polly at the Dollar General Store? Next time you go over there, come and get me. I like to look at all that stuff."

I share her affectation for the Dollar General Store. They have stuff piled everywhere: good stuff, useful stuff, crappy stuff, just everything. Unfortunately, I was not shopping at the Dollar General Store when one of our Glen residents drove through the front doors of the store. It was one of those "Ohhhh dear, I am s-o-o sorry. I must have accidentally stepped on the accelerator when I intended to brake." Imagine... one day you're piddling around in the Dollar General Store looking for Vitamin E lotion and...*BAM! Glass is flying everywhere, and people are running for their lives.* I missed the whole thing. It would have been more entertaining than the French Revolution set to music.

"Speaking of mysteries, Leslie, I may have one for you." Mrs. Towers leaned over the table in earnest.

Belinda's warning voice intoned, "Mrs. Towers..."

"No, Belinda, seriously. You girls know where I get my hair done."

Mrs. Towers drives to a small beauty shop in Clifton where she gets her hair washed and set three times a week. It's about the only driving she does anymore. You don't want to get behind Mrs. Towers' car on hairdo day. Even a preacher would cuss a blue streak if stuck behind our well-coiffed geriatric friend.

"Sure, you still go to Lilly's in town, right?" I encouraged her.

"*Leslie*," my friend warned, but I cut her off. "Go ahead, Mrs. Towers."

"I was so surprised when Lilly told me"—she lowered her voice to a conspiratorial whisper—"prostitutes."

"What? Prostitutes? In the Glen?" Belinda was aghast.

"No, no, not in the Glen. You know that big parking lot next to the furniture store on East Street? Lilly's place is near the furniture store, not too far from Big Lots. I like that Big Lots store. Anyway, Lilly told me that prostitutes hang out in that parking lot at night. That's why she doesn't take evening appointments anymore."

"Why? Prostitutes aren't known for attacking beauty shop owners after dark." I frowned.

"She's not afraid of the prostitutes, Leslie. It's the johns. You know, the men who visit the prostitutes."

I snorted a laugh at Mrs. Towers' vernacular. "I don't believe the men frequenting the parking lot area are interested in attacking Lilly's blue-haired clientele."

"That isn't nice, Leslie. I don't have blue hair," Mrs. Towers scolded.

"No…no…no. Blue hair is slang for…"

"Old ladies?" Our neighborhood matriarch sniffed.

"You know I didn't mean anything by that. Let's get back to the mystery, Mrs. Towers."

In a hushed, conspiratorial voice, she continued, "According to Lilly, one of the girls has gone missing."

Belinda groaned into her hands. "*Oh, this is not good.*"

"Lilly said the prostitutes are all very nice people. They keep the operation very low-key. You know, they don't stand on Main Street in miniskirts and five-inch heels *yoo-hoo*ing at potential customers or anything. Anyway, according to Lilly, the scuttlebutt among the girls is that one of the girls just stopped showing up not too long ago. According to Lilly, they are concerned about her. Right away I thought of you, Leslie."

My friend shook her head and groaned again.

"What's the girl's name?"

"No...no...no."

"Belinda, honey, what's wrong? According to Lilly, they are very nice girls. Nobody deliberately chooses such a profession, you know. We shouldn't judge."

"Don't pay any attention to her, Mrs. Towers. She pretends she doesn't like a good mystery, but she's in denial. What's the hooker's name?"

"I don't like that word."

"What? Hooker? Why?"

"It has a derogatory connotation. It sounds mean. Like blue-haired old ladies seems mean."

"There are other terms for them: prostitutes, ladies of the evening, working girls, etc. Although I *was* a working girl, but I *wasn't* a hooker."

Mrs. Towers pursed her lips with disapproval. "I just don't like that word, Leslie. I don't like low-brow talk."

"How about if we refer to the women as call girls? Would that be acceptable?"

"Yes. That's more genteel."

"Okay then, agreed. From now on the prostitutes and hookers will be referred to as call girls. Now, what's the name of this missing *call girl?*"

"I don't know. Lilly said she didn't know any of the girls by their real names. They all use phony ones, like Daisy or Cocoa—names like that."

"And in the evening they frequent the parking lot next to the furniture store?"

Mrs. Towers nodded. "According to Lilly, yes."

"Hmmmmmm…," I hmmed.

Belinda stood. "Come on, Leslie; I'll make us some coffee at my place."

Mrs. Towers lifted Riff from her lap with both hands and offered her up. Most people can one-hand Riff, but Mrs. Towers is getting along in years.

"Oh, goody! I figured you would cave on the coffee eventually." I jumped up to follow her through the doorway to the patio. Before I slid the door closed behind us, I called out, "Mrs. Towers, can turkeys fly? Belinda says they can't."

"Wild turkeys can fly. They even roost in trees at night. Domestic turkeys are bred for food. They're too fat and heavy to fly, but wild turkeys can scoot around on the ground really fast, and they can fly. I know because Arnie used to go turkey hunting. The meat wasn't worth the effort, but Arnie liked to run around shooting at them. Then he'd hand the scrawny things to me. What a waste of time."

I turned to follow my friend. "Hey, Mrs. Towers said I'm right. Wild turkeys can fly!"

"Turkeys can't fly," she hollered across the lawn.

I trotted away as Mrs. Towers called after us, laughing, "Bye, girls… enjoyed the visit. Let me know what you find out about that missing call girl."

Chapter Two

The only excuse I have for not following up on the missing hooker...um...call girl is that Mrs. Farrow in Unit 7's deliveries sped up significantly, which caught my notice. Mrs. Farrow gets packages daily from every delivery service in existence. It is rather curious. The truth is, I forgot all about the missing call girl until several days later.

I was slurping yet another cup of the aromatic brew as Belinda's allegedly half-feral, long-haired cat slunk around my ankles. As far as I can tell, Butter is more hissing Muppet than ferocious mountain lion. "Hey, let's go for a drive in the country. I don't know about Philadelphia, but you had to be fast in Michigan if you wanted to appreciate the fall colors. The entire state goes from green to white seemingly overnight."

"Philadelphia was pretty in the fall. I don't miss those winters though."

We went back to my place and left Butter to his allegedly half-feral self. I own a white Kia Soul. I love my little car. Belinda doesn't love it, but she doesn't hate it either. *I* hate her car. She drives a black 1998 Riviera. That thing is as big as a pontoon boat. It's pretty funny when you think about it. Here I am driving my hobbit-sized, blond-haired self around in my little white Soul, and there's Belinda—brunette and close to six feet—wheeling around in her black, monster-sized vehicle.

We agreed that a fall-color tour was in order and loaded ourselves into my superior vehicle. We headed north on Trendle Road to an area of the Glen that isn't developed. It's difficult to tell where the Glen stops and the rest of the county takes over. I was buzzing right along, and Belinda had the passenger-side window rolled down so Riff could laugh into the wind.

"Keep a firm hold on her. She isn't a kite."

"I've got her, Les. She loves this!"

"I know. I set up a box fan in the living room for her, but she didn't seem interested in it."

"That's because the fan is stationary. Maybe if you pick it up and run around with it, she'd start laughing. I know I would!"

"Ha-ha-ha." I laughed along with my friend and dog.

The subdivisions dropped away, and we were pretty much heading out into the boonies enjoying the fall colors, Riff blissfully laughing into the wind. We approached the bridge at Mogey Creek, which is the general indicator that you've left the Glen.

"Let's go on a ways, Les; it's so beautiful out here."

So we trundled along on Trendle Road moving farther and farther away from civilization when I saw a roadside stand with a sign proclaiming:

DARE TO TAKE THE CORN MAZE CHALLENGE

HELP THE CLIFTON HIGH BAND GO TO MEMPHIS

$2.50 (INCLUDES CIDER AND DOUGHNUT)

"Want to take the corn maze challenge, Belinda?"

"No, I cannot think of *anything* less challenging than wandering through dead stalks of corn. I wouldn't mind some cider though."

I pulled into the circular driveway of the house where a bunch of teenage kids were manning a table of the promised cider and doughnuts. The house was large and stately. The field of corn was to the right of the house.

A pretty cheerleader-type girl hopped around. "Hi! Want to take the corn maze challenge? All the money is going toward our band outing this spring in Memphis. I'm one of the majorettes."

I used to hate these popular-type girls back in high school. All pretty and peppy with their short little skirts, bouncy ponytails, and clear skin. I had not been one of them. I shook off my failed teenage aspirations. "I don't believe we are up to the corn maze, but we would like some of that cider and a doughnut or two." I set Riff at my feet so I could dig through my purse for some cash.

Two giggling, pretty, and peppy cheerleader/majorette high school girls stopped to squeal over Riff's cuteness and then dashed toward the field and entered the challenging corn maze. Without a moment's hesitation, my little ball of white fur went streaking into the maze after the girls.

"Oh my goodness…Riff…come back!" Gripping my purse in one hand, I raced into the dry stiffness of the cornfield.

The cider table girl called after me, *"Hey, lady, you didn't pay yet!"*

I hollered for Riff, but there was no answering bark and no rocketing ball of white popcorn obediently returning to my side. I trotted down the path of dry, flattened cornstalks until I came to a fork in the road, so to speak. I hollered down each path.

Nothing.

I went right.

After a few minutes of huffing and puffing, I started to feel mildly claustrophobic. That Stephen King movie from the eighties came to mind. The one about some creepy bunch of children living in a cornfield and killing off the adults of the town, or something like that—the specifics of the story eluded me. All I could remember was that the movie had scared the crap out of me.

I kept going until I came to another fork.

I went left.

This path ended in a cul-de-sac of sorts. A mashed-down wide space—a dead end. It reminded me of those crop circles the aliens allegedly leave. A slight rustling noise from behind the cornstalks drew me closer.

"Riff?" I called softly. The rustling came again. Looping my purse strap around one shoulder, I parted the stalks like a curtain. "Riff," I bellowed into the corn…and promptly started to sneeze. Releasing the dried-out stalks, they *thwap*ped together and swayed. From somewhere in my brain encyclopedia, I recalled that there is such a thing as a corn snake. I couldn't recall whether or not it was poisonous. I remember the entire theme song for the *Bozo the Clown* show I watched every Saturday when I was six, but I couldn't recall whether corn snakes were poisonous or not?

Oh man, is there such a thing as a corn spider? If a spider jumps out at me, I will flat-out have a heart attack to rival the one that took my Tom. I backed away from the corn…and sneezed…and sneezed.

From behind me and off to the right or the left—dang cornfield acoustics—I heard Belinda hollering, *"Les-lie, is that you sneezing? Where are you?"*

"I'm over here!" I yelled back…and sneezed.

"Where? Keep sneezing!"

"Heck, I (sneeze) *don't know."* I rummaged through my purse in search of a tissue. Another curiosity surfaced. Why is it when I don't need a tissue, I have to paw through clouds of the things to find my keys or cell phone. But when I need one, I'm lucky to find a single used, dis-gusting wad at the bottom of my purse. I sneezed into the wadded-up tissue and stuck it back into my purse. Another curiosity: I can barely use a public restroom without wrapping the entire room in Saran wrap beforehand, but I will sneeze into the same nasty, wadded-up purse tissue without concern. I suppose because I already own the germs.

I started retracing my steps to the fork and took the opposite path.

She yelled for me again, and we repeated our vaudevillian hollering back-and-forth. I tried hopping up and down, but there was no way I could jump high enough to see over the towering cornstalks. I have never been gymnastically talented at leaping in the air like…well… a cheerleader. Belinda's tall, but even if she could poke her head above the towering corn stalks, I certainly wouldn't see her up there.

Rounding a curve, I faced three separate mashed-down pathways going who knew where. These high school kids were *sadists*.

I went charging down the middle path, breathlessly calling for my dog. Poor Riff. She must be terrified out here in the middle of this rustling, dying forest of corn. The pathway curved and wove all over the place. For the first time, I felt sorry for Eric…lost in the dying, vine-infested potato fields of the Idahoan wilderness.

Finally, I burst through an opening onto the grassy lawn beside the house. Huffing and puffing, I realized that the maze wove around until exiting back onto the grass about fifty feet from the cider and doughnut stand. The girls who had entered the maze ahead of me were waving, and one cuddled my stupid, little brat of a dog.

Belinda came stumbling out about fifteen feet to my right…closer to the roadside stand. The maze must have been designed so that it didn't matter which one of those three paths one selected, they all emptied out onto the lawn.

I stomped down to meet her, grumbling that my blue Keds tennis shoes were covered in dead cornstalk dust. Straightening her glasses, she greeted me, "Oh my, that was rather frightening."

Stomping corn dust from our shoes, we passed two young men at the edge of the cornfield. They were throwing bundles of dried cornstalks into the bed of a truck. One of them waved halfheartedly, and I raised my hand to return the wave but wafted the air in front of my nose instead. The guy didn't even notice. He just hefted another bundle into the back of the truck.

We gave the two men and the truck a wide berth. When we reached the cider table, I gathered Riff into my arms, shaking her paws free of corn dust. Accepting a cup of cider from the initial cheerleader/majorette/whatever, I said, "Whew…those boys are ripe."

She laughed. "Yeah, they must have come from gathering eggs or something."

"Gathering eggs?"

"Yeah, they smell like the henhouse. Seth's mama must have had him cleaning out the chicken coop this morning. She's going to have to hose him down before she lets *him* back in the house."

"You know those boys?"

Initial Cheerleader cheered up, "Yeah. That's Seth Tackett, and Boyd Thicke. They were five years ahead of us in school; not sure either one graduated. Seth's grandfather owns that rundown butcher shop up the road. Daddy lets them take some of the cornstalks for the deer."

"What deer?" I sipped my cider after forking over the required five dollars to cover us both.

"They set up deer blinds and bait the deer with piles of dried corn and stalks. When they get a buck poking around, they blast it from the blind."

I was appalled. "That's terrible! Deer blinds should be illegal. Imagine hiding in a treehouse to blow away Bambi snuffling around a pile of old corn!"

"I'd rather have them hiding out up there than staggering around in the woods shooting each other. That happens every year," Initial Cheerleader opined gravely from her perch on top of the cider/doughnut table.

I called to the girl who had been cuddling Riff before sliding behind the wheel of the car, "Hey! Watch out for corn snakes in there! I hear they can get really big."

All four girls stared back wide-eyed.

Belinda chuckled a scolding. "Leslie, that was mean."

"Serves them right. Running two old ladies around an old field of corn."

$$\bullet \; \bullet \; \bullet$$

Continuing our color tour, we rounded a curve and saw a sign in front of a ramshackle structure.

TACKETT'S FISHING / HUNTING / MEAT PROCESSING

"Oh, Frank told me about this place a long time ago. He came out this way to go deer hunting the first year we moved to the Glen; darned fool almost shot his foot off." After her husband died, Belinda took what was left of him back to Philadelphia. She has two sons and several grandkids there. I can't keep any of them straight. I only have to keep track of one daughter and one granddaughter in Michigan. My granddaughter, Janie, is twenty now and couldn't care less about visiting Grandma. I'm not that broken up about it.

I pulled into the gravel parking lot.

"Why are you pulling in here? This place is a dump."

"I want to check it out. It has character."

"A character disorder, perhaps. You've got to be kidding. I'm not sure this place is even open."

I parked the car and lifted Riff from her lap. "Riff and I are going to scope it out."

"I hate it when you start talking like a Navy SEAL."

I crunched through the dried leaves around the car and met Belinda as she elongated her tall self from the passenger seat muttering, "I'm going to regret this."

A bell jangled as we entered. "See, there's a bell. It's open."

There was a counter with an old-fashioned cash register on one end and a sign hanging above it.

ASK ABOUT A HUNTING OR FISHING LICENSE

"Like I said…this is a store for hunters. Regular people don't come in here." Drifting over to a glass case, Belinda pointed, "See? Fishing lures and stuff. There isn't a thing in here to interest either of us."

I looked at the goofy-looking lures. "Boy, fish must not have very good eyesight," I mumbled at the display of rubber crickets and neon worms. I pointed at a security camera. "He's protecting something more than just fishing lures."

I turned in a circle. "Oooh, and look at that wicked-looking thing!" A hunter's crossbow hung on a far wall. "A person could do some serious damage with that. Remember when Burt Reynolds used one in that movie, what was the name of it? You know the one where there was all that fiddling music in it?"

"I know the one you mean, but I can't remember the name of it either. Anyway, this Mr. Tackett is running a hunting store. Those bow-and-arrow things are used for hunting, and that camera is probably one of those dummy ones." Swiveling her head, she pointed. "See, he's got another one over there. They must be dummies. It would cost a fortune to run a bunch of video around a dumpy little bait store like this."

A door opened at the rear of the store, and a fifty-something man wearing a messy, blood-stained butcher's apron appeared. He raised a hand in greeting, took off the apron, and hung it on a hook next to the doorway he had just exited.

"Welcome, ladies. Something I can help you with?"

Belinda morphed into Scarlet O'Hara, oozing charm. "My friend and I live in the Glen. We were just driving around looking at the lovely fall colors, and we happened to notice this…um…rustic store of yours." She dusted her blouse prissily. "We're simply covered in corn dust. We just came from that corn maze up the road."

The man smiled. "Well, I'm Sam Tackett. My grandsons helped the girls mash down that corn maze." He chuckled. "Those boys had corn dust in their ears for days afterward.

"You ladies go ahead and have a look around. Never know but that you'll see something you might like. I also have game meat in the freezer in the back if you think you might be interested in a venison roast or two."

"Venison?" I asked stupidly.

"Deer meat, Les. Venison is the name for deer meat," Belinda informed me.

"Why isn't it just called deer meat?"

Sam Tackett laughed. "Good question. Now that you mention it, why isn't beef just called cow meat?"

"Exactly." I grinned at Mr. Tackett.

The bell over the front entrance jangled, interrupting our philo-sophical musings. A well-built young man somewhere in his thirties muscled in a wooden crate. He called out cheerily, "Catsup. Get your catsup here!" He sounded like a hot dog vendor at a baseball game. He humped the crate across the store to a long counter and thumped it down mightily.

Mr. Tackett greeted the man, "Hey, Scott, be right with you."

"Excuse me, ladies. I need to sign for this delivery. We carry Papa Field's Catsup," he announced proudly. "Always like to support local businesses."

"By all means, Mr. Tackett, take care of your delivery." As he turned away, I called out a question, "Say, Mr. Tackett, you probably know a lot about turkeys. My friend and I are having a debate about whether or not turkeys can fly. Do you know?"

"Turkeys can't fly, ma'am."

"See, I told you so." Belinda huffed her way down one of the aisles.

"You're sure that wild turkeys can't fly?"

"Oh, *wild turkeys*? Sure, wild turkeys fly. Domestic turkeys are too heavy to get off the ground. Now, if you'll excuse me for a few minutes…"

Papa Field's Catsup has been sold throughout Middle Tennessee since the 1950s and has a distribution center in Clifton. I can get from my house to Clifton in half an hour, but Tackett's store is so far north of the Glen, this fellow must have to drive an hour just to deliver catsup here.

The two men spoke in low voices for a couple of minutes, then Mr. Tackett signed something on a clipboard. The young man took the board and tore off a copy, handing the paper to Mr. Tackett—an invoice I assumed. I found it curious that he would haul all the way up here from Clifton just to deliver a few bottles of catsup. I am a naturally curious and observant person.

Just last summer I found it curious when our eighty-nine-year-old neighbor Abner Cummings, turned up in the scooper bucket of the lake-dredging machine. Even more unusual was his advanced state of submerged deadness, but I digress.

I moseyed over to the counter and pretended to be looking at the soft drink choices in a standing cooler. Noticing my maneuvering, Mr. Tackett called, "Can I get something for you, ma'am?"

"Before we leave, Mr. Tackett, I believe I will purchase one of your Diet Cokes, but we aren't in a hurry. I find your store…quaint. I'm interested in rustic, quaint places." I was talking for the sake of talking. Belinda was wandering up and down the shop aisles. I could see the top of her head every once in a while in between stacks of stuff on the shelves.

The young man spoke loudly. "Sam, I have your other delivery around back. Could you help me unload it? Won't take but a few minutes."

Mr. Tackett looked at me uncertainly. I assured him, "Oh, please, Mr. Tackett, go ahead; we'll amuse ourselves."

"Well, okay," and then to the young man, "Come on, Scott, we'll go out the back."

The two men walked to the rear of the store and exited through the same doorway Mr. Tackett had appeared from earlier. I heard them talking and clomping down the hallway and then the opening and slamming of an outside door.

I scurried over to the door that had a clear window in the top half. As I stood peering down the utilitarian-looking hallway that ran the back length of the store, I noticed a couple of chest freezers along the far wall and two more security cameras. The freezers reminded me of the one my grandmother had on her farm in Kentucky. Granny used to go headfirst into that freezer pawing through frozen chickens and whatnot in search of whatever. I realized while I was looking through the window in the door that I could also see through a larger window directly across the hall. Through the larger window I could see the back lot where the catsup guy had his catsup truck. Catsup guy was opening the double doors in the back of his truck when Mr. Tackett motored up in a little, bitty truck.

Scurrying into the center of the store, I hollered, "Belinda! Come here!"

"Where are you?" she hollered back.

I flapped my arm up and down until I was sure she had seen me.

Hurrying to my side, she said, "Leslie, Mr. Tackett has three shelves stocked with Papa Field's Catsup over there. How much catsup can he sell way out here?"

"I don't know," I whispered; "come and tell me what you see."

I opened the door to the back hallway, and Belinda followed, muttering, "We probably shouldn't be back here."

Belinda stood next to me, and we stared out the window. Mr. Tackett and catsup guy were wrestling a large something out of the delivery truck.

"Whatever that thing is, it ain't catsup." We watched the two men transfer the blue-tarp-covered, lumpy something from the back of the truck onto Sam's little toy utility truck. They were having a hard time with the lumpy bundle because whatever it was kept shifting and rolling.

"What is that?" Belinda wondered aloud.

"I don't know, but I can tell you what it looks like."

"Don't start. You see body bags everywhere we go. The catsup man delivers store stuff. That's all you need to know. Wait a minute. Now where are they going? I have to admit, this is a little odd."

Belinda is always in mystery denial.

Mr. Tackett was in the driver's seat of the little utility truck, catsup guy in the seat beside him, and the something loaded onto the little, bitty truck bed. The little truck sped off toward the back of the property on a dirt trail and past a prefabricated barn-like structure—one of those structures made out of pressed metal.

I mumbled into the glass, "I hate it when I get behind one of those little Tonka Toy trucks the maintenance people drive around the Glen. They never go more than twenty miles an hour."

"Here." I shoved Riff into her arms. I sometimes feel bad about tossing Riff around like a sweater. "I want to get a look at that invoice."

A warning whine followed me. "Leslie…"

"You watch for them." I swung back through the connecting door and hurried behind the counter where I had seen Mr. Tackett stuff the paper after he had signed it. I was amazed at what I found.

I hollered, "Belinda, come look at this setup."

Trotting up to the counter she huffed, "What?"

"Come around and look at this."

Her eyes went wide when she rounded the corner. "Oh my, this looks like a very elaborate system." Sam Tackett had a regular casino-type security system rigged up beneath the counter, with several monitors showing various sections of the store, including the hallway in the back.

"Look, Belinda, motion sensors…zones one, two, and three. Motion sensors just like Perfect Polly. You know, when it senses motion, an alarm goes off somewhere."

"I know what motion sensors are, Les. These are a tad more sophisticated than your As Seen On TV chirping parakeet." I started moving papers around. "What are you looking for?"

"The invoice that fella handed to Sam; here it is: one case of twelve bottles of Papa Field's Catsup delivered by one Scott Epperling. That's a long way to drive just to deliver twelve bottles of catsup."

"Yeah, especially when Sam already has three full shelves of catsup. And, why would he have such an elaborate security system? So what if somebody shoplifts a bottle of catsup. She smacked her forehead with her free hand. "Now you have *me* imagining dastardly deeds everywhere. Let's get out of here."

Once in a while my mind wanders down a hallway without an exit. "Personally, I buy the generic Foods tuff City brand of catsup. I believe catsup is pretty much catsup…but, I could be wrong. Maybe Papa Field's Catsup contains some secret ingredient like Kentucky Fried Chicken." I turned off my wandering dialogue. "Let's not leave yet; let's go see if they've come back yet."

We returned to the back hallway and stood side by side at the window. I mumbled, "Nothing but Scott's truck. They must still be behind that building, off-loading whatever was in that tarp. I wonder what's behind that building. Heck, I wonder what's *in* that building?"

"I don't care about that building. You're making up stuff just to drive me crazy. You always imagine convoluted shenanigans going on whenever you get bored. You need to join a social club, take up Pickleball or something. You know you could use the exercise *and* the socialization."

"I already take line dancing."

"One hour, one day a week, two-stepping around a gym and giggling is not exercise or socialization."

I ignored her. "They've been gone a long time. I'm going to look around and see what he's keeping in these big chest freezers."

"Well, I'm not standing guard while you snoop. I hope he catches you on his security cameras and has you arrested for trespassing."

"It isn't trespassing, Belinda. The man told us to look around."

"He didn't suggest we take a tour of his storeroom or check out his invoices."

"Hey, you're the one who noticed that the man is already floating in catsup. Go back into the store. I can handle this."

I didn't watch to see where she went but walked down the hallway to where one of those large chest freezers stood. I muscled up the lid to examine the contents and stared in at a bunch of bundles of meat wrapped in butcher paper with scribbling across the front of each one. I allowed the door to drop with a bang. Then I moved down to the second freezer and repeated the process. I didn't find anything except lumps of frozen meat. I dropped the freezer door with a loud bang and surveyed my surroundings. I walked toward a massive steel door with a big crank-like handle on it: a walk-in freezer.

That's a lot of freezer space for a little backwoods butcher-catsup store.

I grabbed the handle with both hands and gave it a mighty yank. I was surprised that it wasn't locked. I backstepped and hauled the big door open. Vaporous fog floated from the open freezer. At first I just poked my head inside, but there was such a strong tugging sensation from that non-exit hallway in my brain that I found myself stepping inside. It wasn't a huge space. I estimated it to be about six feet deep and five feet wide. I could almost stretch out in the widthwise, and Belinda could handle the depth. I took a couple of tentative steps and wondered why on earth Sam Tackett had boxed crates of Papa Field's Catsup in his walk-in freezer. On a shelf beneath the catsup were plastic sandwich bags with lumps of something in them. It just looked like little baggies of ice to me.

Mr. Tackett's firm voice scared an inward snort from my throat.

"What in the world are you doing in there?"

I whirled around in the misty freezer, feeling light-headed. "Oh, you scared me!" I started to babble, which is what I do when I don't know what else to do. "You were gone for so long. I was looking for those roasts you were talking about earlier, and..."

Sam Tackett offered his hand. "Lady, come on out of there. I'll get the roasts for you."

Belinda's piercing scream erupted all around us. I bolted from the freezer past Sam in the direction of her scream. I heard the *wump* of the freezer door closing behind me and was halfway down the hallway when she staggered through some swinging doors near the end. Glasses dangling from one hand, she had her face buried in Riff's fur.

Rushing to my best friend, I gasped, "Belinda, what's wrong? Are you all right?"

She lifted her head and worked her mouth, managing only a few pathetic gurgles. She gave a halfhearted wave toward the double swinging doors and buried her face again in Riff's ruff.

Sam hollered, "Don't go in there!"

Well, of course I had to. I went barreling through the doors and ran into a wall of *smell*. The stench was like a living thing: dense and determined. My eyes began to water, and I threw my arms up in front of me in a defensive stance. Through the fog I could make out the body of a large animal hanging by its hind legs from some overhead contraption. The thing looked huge, like a moose, but we don't have moose around here. Of course, I hadn't known we had bears either until this summer. This animal had to be a large deer. It looked monstrous hanging there, like something out of a medieval torture chamber. There was a bucket next to the hanging carcass and a heavy wooden table with knives and such on it. Using my hands as a filter, I sucked in my breath and pedaled backward, right into Sam Tackett.

He grabbed my arm, and I started hopping around, going "Gah... ah-ah-ah," slapping at his hands.

"It's okay," he said soothingly. "Come on out of there." I allowed him to pull me into the hallway, where Belinda had recovered somewhat. "You ladies shouldn't go wandering around like that, barging into freezers and everything," he scolded. "We do the meat processing back here. It's in the back for a reason, you know. If you're not expecting it, it can be upsetting...especially for ladies like you."

He was actually very kind. After all, we had both been snooping around his establishment without permission.

"I-I'm sorry, Mr. Tackett," Belinda stammered. "Sam, I really am."

Fleetingly I thought Belinda sounded as if she was quoting from a book by Dr. Seuss. "Me too," I gulped.

"Here," he said, "come on into the store and sit down for a while. I'll get you some water."

We followed obediently and sat down in a couple of chairs near the counter. Sam opened a cooler and withdrew two bottles of cold water. We accepted the water gratefully.

"Boy, that was a shock," I admitted. "Why is it hanging up there like that?"

"It's the first part of deer processing." He gave a rueful laugh. "The part you aren't supposed to see."

I found myself warming to the man until I recalled that blue-tarp-covered, saggy, lumpy bundle of something.

"Are you ladies sure you're okay now? Do you still want the roasts?"

"The roasts? Oh yeah, the roasts. Yes, of course. Do you have a couple of four-pound roasts?" I stammered, having no idea how big a four-pound roast would be.

"Sure. You ladies rest for a bit, and I'll bring them right out."

Sam walked back toward the door that led to the hallway, that led to the freezers, which led to Bambi's torture chamber.

"I don't want any deer meat!" Belinda muttered through gritted teeth. "I may have become a vegetarian today!"

"We can't refuse them now. It will look strange."

"What I saw back there *was* weird!" She huffed and then trembled. "And, good golly, that stench!"

"I know," I admitted. "I've always heard the odor of blood described as sweet and cloying…but that was like being trapped inside the gut of a monster. It was like…"

"All right, that's enough. You made your point."

Sam returned from the back, and we stood to meet him. He had two small, wrapped bundles. When Belinda made no effort to open her purse, I sighed and handed Sam my Visa debit card. After swiping the card and signing the receipt, I accepted the plastic bag that now contained two small venison roasts.

"Thank you, Sam. It was nice to meet you. I'm sorry if we caused you any trouble," I offered.

"Yes…sorry," Belinda echoed.

"No problem. Come back and see us." He smiled a toothy farewell.

I had wanted to quiz him some more about his meat-processing operation, but Belinda was pushing her way out of the store with Riff still in her arms.

"Slow down," I called after her.

She stomped angrily toward the passenger-side door. "I swear I'm in shock." Settling into the passenger seat, she shivered and massaged her eyes behind the lenses of her glasses. "Seeing that poor deer dangling there like that was just so sad. Where is that little bowl you keep for Riff? She could probably use some of this water. The poor little thing is shivering. Speaking of shivering, what were you doing looking in freezers?"

Belinda rooted around in the back of the car for Riff's plastic bowl, which she promptly filled with water, and set it and Riff on the floor at her feet. Riff was happily slurping and slopping water all over the car mat and didn't look the least bit upset to me as I got comfortable in the driver's seat.

I told her about the two chest freezers and the walk-in.

"Leslie! You could have been trapped in that walk-in freezer or tumbled headfirst into a chest freezer. You're such a little shrimp; you'd probably fit too. You had no business snooping around and taking chances like that!"

"Look who's talking. I didn't tell you to go snooping and blundering around that sadomasochistic playroom for Santa's reindeer! You ran us out of there so fast I didn't even get to ask Sam any questions about why he stocks so much Papa Field's Catsup. There were a ton of catsup crates in that walk-in." I frowned. "I didn't see any big, lumpy, blue tarps, just some little bags of ice. You screamed before I could thoroughly investigate the freezer contents."

"Well, thank goodness for that."

"I know you don't want to speculate on what was in the blue tarp, but you have to admit that the shape resembled a body bag."

"Stop it, Les…just stop it! Anyway, body bags are black."

"Nuh-uh, I looked it up."

"Of course you did. I refuse to get caught up in another one of your diabolical murder theories. Everything that looks the least bit curious does not imply murder. I admit those two men looked odd trundling across the back forty with that blue-tarp-covered bundle of whatever. And Sam Tackett seems to have some kind of hoarding disorder when it comes to Papa Field's Catsup, but that is none of our business."

Riff had finished her water and was sitting on Belinda's foot, so she one-handed her into her lap. "Mr. Tackett runs a butcher shop for game animals. For all we know they could have been hauling a bag of squirrels in that blue tarp!"

I barked a loud laugh. "Squirrels! You saw the size of that bag. You could have put two hundred squirrels in there. Not only that, but that Scott guy is driving a catsup truck, not a meat wagon."

"Why are you laughing?"

"I don't know; for some reason a big bag of squirrels just struck me as funny."

Lifting my dog to her lips, she kissed the top of her head. "Riff, we may as well run off and join the circus! Your mama is crazy."

We rode in silence for a bit when I suddenly remembered the name of the Burt Reynolds movie. "*Deliverance!*" I thumped the steering wheel. "That was the name of that movie."

"I've heard that music in my head ever since you mentioned it. Only, I'm pretty sure it was banjos and not fiddles."

Chapter Three

Leaving our corn-dust-covered shoes in the garage, I invited Belinda in for a Diet Coke. Riff stuck her nose in her bowl of kibble while my friend went to the refrigerator for our drinks. The message light was blinking on the kitchen phone, so I punched the button to hear Mrs. Towers' blubbery voice. "Leslie, I can't find Jane Doe anywhere. In fact, I haven't seen her since the day you and Belinda were here. John, her buddy, has been around, but the poor thing looks lost. I'm afraid something has happened to Jane. Call me when you get in." She ended on a half sob.

Having heard the message, Belinda said, "Uh-oh."

I phoned Mrs. Towers and promised we would come down to see her. An obviously distraught Mrs. Towers was waiting for us at the front door. "Something has happened to Jane. I just know it. She and her pal have been around my place every day for weeks!"

Clucking and patting Mrs. Towers, we encouraged her to take a seat at her kitchen table. I dropped Riff onto her lap, hoping that petting Riff would calm her down.

Belinda frowned. "Leslie and I were here three days ago, Mrs. Towers. You haven't seen Jane since?"

"That's right. I called the Safety Department to see if anybody had hit a deer with their car, but none were reported. I even called the Wildlife Resources people, and they said they weren't aware of any—" she did one of those sobbing gulps— "carcasses found along any of the roads in the Glen. Jane wasn't able to go very far because of her disability. I can't imagine what has happened to her! Leslie, you have to do something."

Belinda looked hurt. "Why does Leslie have to do something? What do you think she can do?"

"She's good at this investigative stuff. Why do you think I told her about Lilly's missing call girl?"

Uh-oh. I had forgotten all about the call girl. I stammered, "Belinda and I stumbled onto a suspicious situation too. We haven't had time to look into the missing call girl yet, but we will." As further obfuscation, I rushed headlong into a description of our visit to Sam Tackett's place. "Mrs. Towers, have you ever heard of a place north of the Glen that's run by a man by the name of Sam Tackett? He has a dumpy little bait shop place with a security system elaborate enough for Caesar's Palace!"

"Leslie," Belinda warned.

"Mrs. Towers may find this interesting. Anyway, this Tackett fella runs a sort of hunting-and-fishing supply shop and butchers game animals. Belinda remembers Frank telling her about the place. It's not a large store, looks like a dump actually. He even has motion sensors set up—you know, those laser lights that set off alarms when they're tripped, along the same line as Perfect Polly, only a lot more sophisticated."

"I don't recall ever having seen the place, Leslie. I don't usually drive anywhere except into town to get my hair done. You really need to look into what has happened to that missing girl. Lilly is quite worried."

I pretended I hadn't heard her mildly scolding tone. "Sam Tackett already had three shelves full of Papa Field's Catsup and a delivery guy delivered another case while we were wandering around the store. We just happened upon the place while we were out looking at the fall colors. Then the men went around back, and the delivery guy pulled something large out of his truck, and… Um, why do you suppose Mr. Tackett is stocking his place with so much catsup? Belinda wandered into the business end of the butcher shop when I wasn't watching and discovered a deer strung up by its hind legs." I trailed off. I didn't mention my foray into the freezer.

Belinda huffed, "Well…you…"

Mrs. Towers interrupted. "They hang up the deer so the blood drains from the carcass. Arnie used to hunt. I never cared much for the taste of venison. As far as the catsup overstock goes, maybe this Mr. Tackett is planning a big sale on Papa Field's Catsup. Coincidentally, Papa Field's Catsup has a distribution center behind Main Street, across from that big parking lot next to the furniture store on East Street where the call girls hang out at night. When are you going to look for that girl? Lilly says they don't have enough streetlights downtown. It isn't safe for those girls to be out there like that."

"They aren't supposed to be out there at all, Mrs. Towers. Prostitution is against the law," Belinda said, stating the obvious.

"It's legal in Las Vegas," I pointed out in an effort at edification. "That is good to know though about the Papa Field's Catsup place. Maybe I can ask them some questions about the missing girl."

"Leslie," Belinda warned.

"In fact, I wonder if there is some connection between Papa Field's, Sam Tackett, and this missing call girl."

Mrs. Towers flapped her arms. "None of that has anything to do with Jane Doe. What are we going to do?"

"I can't solve all these mysteries at the same time. I suppose we could go look for Jane in the woods. But, if she's injured or something, we won't be able to do anything about it." I didn't like having to admit that there wasn't anything I, or Belinda, could do about this missing-deer situation. I couldn't stand the crestfallen look on Mrs. Towers' face. "We'll go down to the Safety Department and see if we can get Quinn to send some of his guys to walk through the woods." I looked at my friend beseechingly. "Right, Belinda? The way I see it, the police owe us a couple of favors!"

Belinda nodded energetically. "Sure, that's a good idea. Quinn will look into Jane's disappearance."

"And we can ask him whether he knows anything about Lilly's missing call girl," I added triumphantly.

Mrs. Towers objected. "No, Leslie, you have to look into Lilly's missing call girl on the down-low. Belinda is right; prostitution is against the law. I don't want to get those girls in trouble."

She practically tossed Riff into my arms. "Take Riff. I'm going with you. I'm worried to death about Jane Doe. She's such a small, little thing. I doubt she's much more than a year old!"

There was no talking her out of it, so I ran home to get my Soul. We loaded Mrs. Towers and her walker into the backseat, with Belinda and Riff riding shotgun.

The minute we entered the Safety Department building, Mrs. Towers took over, angrily stumping across the lobby toward one of Quinn's deputies, Mark Edwards.

"Young man, I need to speak with Sheriff Braddock right away." Mrs. Towers stopped in front of the officer, practically barking at the man, who, despite Mrs. Towers' description of "young man," was probably in his midsixties. Age is relative.

Holding Riff under one arm, I minced up beside Mrs. Towers. "Officer Edwards, isn't it?"

"Yes, ma'am. I'm Officer Mark Edwards. Is there something I can do for you, ladies?"

"You can get the sheriff!" Mrs. Towers barked again.

Officer Edwards suppressed a grin. "Chief Braddock is out on call, ma'am, but he's on his way back in if you all want to wait." He said "you all" like a Yankee. I know because I'm a Yankee, and that's how I say it.

Mrs. Towers glared at Edwards as if it was his fault that Chief Braddock was not on the immediate premises. The three of us bumbled around the lobby for a bit. Mrs. Towers finally lowered herself into a chair to wait, while Belinda and I walked over to peruse the bulletin board.

A prominently displayed notice caught my eye. "Look. Hunting season is starting. Not guns but those bow-and-arrow things, you know, crossbows, like Burt Reynolds in that *Deliverance* movie."

Belinda widened her eyes and scrunched down level with my face, and whispered, "Are you suggesting that a hunter is responsible for Jane's disappearance? You know hunting isn't allowed in the Glen. Besides, according to this notice, the season doesn't even start until next week."

"I'm not suggesting anything...yet. I'm just running some theories around in my brain."

"Be careful with that, Les. I know your brain. There's a lot to trip over in there."

"Very funny. I can't get the picture of that deer carcass hanging in Sam Tackett's butcher shop out of my mind."

"Neither can I." She shivered. "It was horrible!"

I teased, "You were a big-time ER nurse in Philadelphia. I'm surprised you're not made of sterner stuff."

"Most of my patients weren't dangling from the ceiling when I tended to them." Belinda is a very sensitive woman. I was glad to hear the sarcasm in her voice. I took it as a sign that she was over the horrors we'd encountered out at Tackett's.

"You didn't notice whether that deer—the one that was hanging in the butcher shop—had any, um, lady parts? Did you?"

She gaped at me googgly-eyed.

"I guess not," I answered myself.

"Sheriff Braddock, I need to see you about a very serious matter!" Mrs. Towers' strident voice carried across the lobby. Whirling about, we saw Mrs. Towers accosting Quinn, who'd just entered the building.

Mrs. Towers was struggling to stand with the aid of her walker, and Quinn reached out to steady her. "Mrs. Towers, is everything all right out your way?"

Belinda and I hurried over to them, and I transferred Riff to my other arm. "Quinn, we have a situation that requires immediate attention."

"Jane Doe is missing," Mrs. Towers announced, "and we need your men to search the woods for her."

"Jane Doe? You actually know someone by the name of Jane Doe?" He couldn't stop the grin from crossing his face.

Belinda cut in. "Jane Doe is a deer, Quinn…a little, young, crippled doe. She's been a regular visitor at our townhomes, and she's so docile Mrs. Towers has practically made a pet out of her. Anyway, her companion, John Doe, is still coming around, but Jane hasn't been seen for three days."

Quinn looked at our faces one by one and shook his head. "So, you want to file a missing person's report on a deer? Do I understand you all correctly?"

"Well, yes, actually, Quinn…all we are asking is for a couple of your guys to walk the woods around our place and see whether you can find her. Mrs. Towers already called here, and also the Wildlife Resource place to rule out whether she's been hit by a car or anything." Belinda can let her voice go all girly and flirty-coy. I don't have that talent.

Her feminine talents didn't seem to be working, because Quinn lectured, "Ladies, I cannot use our manpower to chase wayward, pet deer. They are wild animals; you shouldn't be trying to domesticate them in the first place."

Mrs. Towers drew to her full height—approximately five foot

three—and attempted to stretch even higher by standing on her tiptoes while using the walker as support. "Sheriff Braddock, I do *not* make a habit of domesticating wild animals. Son, this is a little bitty, young, crippled doe. She is not one of these healthy deer that go bounding and leaping all over the place. She can barely walk. Now, either you have a couple of your men walk around our woods a bit or we will do it ourselves. I doubt you want an eighty-five-year-old woman who is dependent on a walker tramping around in the forest!"

Quinn looked at Mrs. Towers helplessly. "Well, do you?" she repeated firmly.

With a big sigh, Quinn acquiesced. "No ma'am, I don't want the three of you tramping around out there. A couple of us will drive out your way and have a look around."

"When?" Mrs. Towers is not a woman to be trifled with, one of the reasons she is so talented at ferreting out relevant bits of information on issues critical to the Glen.

"Officer Edwards and I will take a ride over there now. Would that be soon enough for you, Mrs. Towers?" That last bit had a sarcastic bent to it that did not set well with Mrs. Towers.

"Don't get smart with me, Sheriff. All we are asking is for you and your men to do your jobs." She sniffed.

"Actually, deer fall under the jurisdiction of the Wildlife Resource Agency." When he saw Mrs. Towers starting to puff up all over again, he quickly amended, "But we are glad to come out and take a look around. If we find your wounded animal, we'll call the Wildlife Resource Agency to come and take care of it."

"Sheriff, if you find Jane, I expect you to let me know about it before you ask the Wildlife people to 'take care' of her."

"Yeah," I quipped defiantly, "we are all aware how they 'take care' of the bears around here!"

"Leslie and I will wait for you at Mrs. Towers' place. We appreciate anything you can do for us." She'd gone all girly-coy again.

Belinda and I, still carrying Riff, walked through the lobby toward the exit. Mrs. Towers followed us, clomping her walker down and hauling her body behind it. "I thought that went well, don't you girls?"

Rolling my eyes, I placed my arm on Belinda's to get her to pause. Handing Riff to her, I whispered, "Take Riff and Mrs. Towers back to the car. I want to ask Quinn some questions."

"About what?" Belinda asked in her normal Belinda voice.

Mrs. Towers clomped and called over her shoulder, "Come on, Belinda. Leslie wants to ask Quinn something, and she doesn't want us to know what it is."

Nothing wrong with Mrs. Towers' hearing.

"Go ahead, I'll just be a minute."

She huffed, adjusted Riff in her arms, and trailed Mrs. Towers.

Quinn had disappeared through the make-believe doorway that separates the lobby from the offices. The doorway illusion is simply a break where the freestanding wall partitions end and the space runs into a wall. I rounded the corner of the make-believe doorway and spied Quinn chatting with Officer Edwards.

Approaching the two men, I asked, "Sheriff, oh, I mean Chief. Sorry, Mrs. Towers has apparently been rubbing off on me."

Chuckling, Quinn said, "That's okay, Mrs. Barrett. I kind of like it when people call me 'sheriff.'"

Officer Edwards added with a grin, "Yeah, the only moniker he likes better is 'marshall.'"

Still chuckling, Quinn asked, "What can I help you with?"

I waved my arm in a vague gesture toward the lobby area. "I noticed on the bulletin board that hunting season in our county is about to begin."

Quinn nodded. "That's correct...for archery and crossbows. You ladies don't need to be concerned about that. There's no hunting allowed in the Glen."

"Yes, well...I was wondering whether you have ever encountered... um, poaching or illegal hunting or shanghaiing in the Glen?"

Quinn frowned. "Shanghai? Isn't that a city in China? Anyway, there haven't been any reports of poaching in the Glen."

Officer Edwards added his two cents. "Shanghai is also a verb."

Quinn gave him the evil eye, and Edwards noticed. "He means there haven't been any poaching incidents in the heart of the Glen. Every year there are one or two incidents reported in the outlying areas. I've been with the Glen force for five years, three years longer than Quinn."

Quinn didn't appear to suffer any affront from his subordinate's voluntary tutorial. "That's true, Mrs. Barrett, but the Glen is so much more developed than in years past that any willful hunting on Glen property has virtually ceased."

"But it could happen, unwillfully?"

"Well, yes. Possibly on the northern boundaries of the Glen that haven't been developed. You don't have anything to worry about in your area. Besides, hunters only shoot the bucks, never does."

"I trust you, Quinn, but I don't believe you should be so quick to write off the poaching thing."

He opened his mouth to comment, but I plowed onward. "If somebody would be as unscrupulous as to poach deer in the Glen, what makes you think they wouldn't shoot does? Deer meat is deer meat after all, or venison, I mean."

"I can't dispute your logic, but Mark and I have to look at historical evidence. There haven't been any poaching incidents in several years. Still, I understand that you ladies are concerned about Jane Doe." He couldn't help smirking.

"Mrs. Towers is concerned, Quinn. Belinda and I are simply being supportive."

"Mark and I will run over to your complex in a few minutes. We'll walk the wooded areas and come by Mrs. Towers' unit after we've had a look around. Try to reassure her. I'm sure her doe is all right."

I turned to go but decided to ask Quinn one more question. "Hey, do you guys have any idea what's going on with Mrs. Farrow in Unit 7?"

Quinn leaned back and frowned. "Why? What's wrong with Mrs. Farrow?"

"The woman receives packages every day of the week. UPS, Federal Express, Pony Express, you name it; they pull up to her unit. It's very curious."

Quinn and Mark said they didn't know anything about Mrs. Farrow's odd assembly line of packages, so I left them to their policing and slid into the driver's seat of the Soul.

"What did you need to ask the sheriff, Leslie? I hope you didn't mention Lilly's call girl, and you need to give it a rest about that bear. Everybody is tired of talking about that bear."

"I wasn't asking Quinn about bears or missing call girls, Mrs. Towers. I was asking about the restrictions on hunters. Oh, and I asked him about Mrs. Farrow. He doesn't know anything about what's going on with her either."

"You don't suspect Jane has been cut down by some jackass hunter, do you? How big was that deer carcass you saw out at that bait shop place?" Mrs. Towers has a colorful vocabulary, surpassed only by my late husband's. *Colorful* is too tame a word to describe the in-house dialogue that goes on in an auto plant.

"No, Quinn assured me there haven't been any incidents of deer hunting in the Glen for years. The county hunting season doesn't even start for another week. I was only eliminating it as a possible explanation for Jane's sudden absence. And that deer out at Tackett's place was humongous. Way bigger than Jane Doe."

"I feel better about Jane now that you're looking into the matter, Leslie. You have a natural talent for investigative work."

Belinda one-handed Riff into the backseat. "Leslie, Riff is starting to put on weight. I think you are feeding her too much."

I sighed because I could tell where this was going. "She went in last week for a checkup and toenail trim. She weighs ten pounds, and the vet said she was at least two pounds overweight."

"I thought so," said Belinda, *the all-knowing health expert.*

"I've cut back on her wet food, and Riff's not too happy about it."

"She needs exercise, Leslie; you both do."

Mrs. Towers chuckled. She's heard this discourse a million times. "Don't start with me, Belinda. I have increased our walks. We now walk the length of the complex and then again down by the boardwalk and all the way back."

"Yeah, and how much of that walk does Riff spend nestled in your arms?"

"Belinda, look at Riff. She's just a little bitty thing. By the time we walk that circuit, I'm exhausted. What do you want me to do, drag Riff's limp little body behind me across the boardwalk?"

I glanced in the rearview mirror to see Mrs. Towers and Riff in the backseat. Riff was panting happily at the conversation, undoubtedly because she kept hearing her name. Mrs. Towers met my eye with a grin. It pleased me that we'd been able to take her mind off Jane's dilemma for a few minutes.

Chapter Four

Ensconced around the kitchen table, we returned to the question of the missing Jane Doe while Riff happily slopped water all over the floor from a cereal bowl that Mrs. Towers sacrificed for her thirsty pleasure.

Mrs. Towers' voice quivered. "I cannot imagine what might have happened to her. She and John have been regular as clockwork."

I tried to lighten the mood with a legitimate question. "Hey, how come you named her companion John? Did you check out his gentleman parts?"

"Leslie, Riff is sitting on your foot," she said.

"I know." I used both hands to haul the fat-butt fur ball onto my lap.

"And in answer to your question, no I didn't need to get a look at John's *junk*." Mrs. Towers grinned through her tears.

Belinda responded with her bark-laugh. "Junk? Wherever did you come up with that one?"

"My twelve-year-old grandson, last summer... Kevin had just climbed out of the water over at Draid's Pool, and he walked toward his mother and me with a hand at his crotch. When he got close enough to hear me, I scolded, 'Kevin, don't manhandle yourself like that in public.' Guess what he said to me. 'Grandma, I was just settling my junk.'"

We all had a good laugh over that one.

"So," I burbled, "if you never got a look at Jane's friend's junk, how do you know that he's a he?"

"Simple, male deer have antlers, females don't."

"Well, they might not have antlers," Belinda giggled, "but girls have junk too!"

Mrs. Towers giggled. "Yes, we certainly do. Some of our junk might be rustier than others, but we still have it! Anyway, Jane owns the name. She's such a sweetheart, I hope she's okay."

The front doorbell rang out, but before Belinda could get up to answer it, Mrs. Towers bellowed, "Come on in, Sheriff!"

The two men entered, hats in hand. "Well, Mrs. Towers, Mark and I have tramped all through your woods, and we didn't find a wounded or deceased doe. We did startle a couple of deer. Maybe one of them was Jane."

With a wobbly voice Mrs. Towers said, "No, Jane can't run. She hobbles. You would've noticed. Sheriff, do you believe it's possible a boat hit Jane? Maybe while swimming in the lake? After what happened to Abner Cummings."

Setting Riff on her feet, I leaned over the table. "I doubt that, Mrs. Towers. Those pontoon boats don't go fast enough to do any real damage anyway." The lakes in the Glen are designated no-wake; trailing bubble streams are *not* allowed.

"I suppose not," she concurred.

• • •

The following morning, Belinda *yoo-hoo*ed her way through the front door, and Riff met her in the foyer. "I'm in the den!" I called.

She rounded the corner already talking. "Leslie, the UPS truck…" I had my binoculars trained on the brown truck parked in front of Unit 7. "Oh, obviously you just saw that great, big box delivered to Mrs. Farrow."

I paused in my surveillance to frown in her direction. "I couldn't make out what it said on the box, could you?"

She came to stand beside me at the window. "I didn't notice."

Resuming my surveillance, I muttered, "Watching UPS delivery people is like watching paint dry."

"FedEx came by forty-five minutes ago. You know, Leslie, you shouldn't snoop on your neighbors with binoculars."

Tom gave them to me after I'd waxed eloquent about yellow finches. Tom was always trying to get me interested in something, anything, probably so he wouldn't feel guilty spending hours whacking stupid, little white balls all over the place. I saw that yellow finch, and the next thing you know I was the proud owner of a book about Tennessee birds and a nifty pair of binoculars. I never opened the bird book, but the rest of his gift has proven to be a useful tool.

"Belinda, you're perfectly capable of buying a pair of your own. Better yet, the Dollar General carries those binocular-type glasses. You've seen them on TV. Those goofy-looking glasses allow you to zoom right up an eagle's nose. Get a pair of those and then you won't have to run over here to find out what's going on over at Mrs. Farrow's. They're only nine ninety-nine. I didn't buy any because I have these. *And*, do not confuse neighborly concern with snoopiness. I'm just naturally curious about the ongoing oddity of daily delivery trucks pulling up to Unit 7. Mrs. Farrow could be in some kind of distress. She moved in two years ago, and nobody seems to know anything about her. The lady is a mystery. According to Mrs. Towers, she doesn't attend any of the neighborhood parties."

"You don't attend any of the neighborhood parties."

"That's different."

"How is it different?"

"It just is. Not only that, but she didn't come to Abner's memorial service at the Baptist church, and she lived right next door to the man."

"Leslie, you wouldn't have gone to Abner's memorial if I hadn't insisted."

"Still, I did attend. Mrs. Farrow did not."

I thought Methodists prayed a lot until Abner's service at the Baptist church. I think *God* may have nodded off during that service. I grew up Methodist but converted to Catholic when Tom and I married. I was never very good at either one. Unless a religion has some pizzazz, I start to count windows or beams in the ceiling.

"You know, wondering what's in those deliveries has given me an idea."

"Uh-oh. It isn't any of our business why she gets so many deliveries. Maybe she's a collector of priceless artifacts or something."

"No, really, listen. We both thought something hinky was going on out at Sam Tackett's with that catsup guy. Why was Scott Epperling delivering Papa Field's Catsup when Sam was already overrun with it? He even had it stacked in that walk-in freezer. Crates of the stuff with 'PAPA FIELD'S' printed all over them. They don't make anything except catsup, so why did Scott ask Sam to help him with his *other* delivery, and what was rolled up in that blue tarp?"

"Scott could have been delivering more catsup around back, Les. Like Mrs. Towers suggested, maybe Sam was planning to run a sale on Papa Field's Catsup…or maybe Sam was asking Scott to help him move something. Just a favor for a friend. Whatever was wrapped up in that tarp obviously took two men to move it."

I gave an inelegant snort. "Yeah, right. Sam Tackett's running a catsup sale for all five people who live north of the Glen. Answer me this: Why was that blue-tarp-covered lump in the Papa Field's delivery truck in the first place? And, it was *Scott* who asked *Sam* to help him, not the other way around. What if Epperling is using his delivery truck for nefarious purposes."

"Define *nefarious* and, what does Scott Epperling and Sam Tackett have to do with Mrs. Farrow?"

"I didn't say the mysteries were connected. However, speculating about what's behind Mrs. Farrow's frequent deliveries caused me to wonder about why Scott Epperling was delivering more catsup to Sam when he was swimming in the stuff. What if Epperling is hauling unlawful stuff around along with those crates of catsup and then delivering it to Sam Tackett using the catsup deliveries as a cover? You know I don't believe in coincidences. We just happen to stumble on something weird going on out at Tackett's place, something involving a catsup delivery driver, and now Jane Doe has gone missing. On top of that we've learned that those call girls hang out near the catsup place, and one of them is missing. All we have to do is follow the obvious clues. Just like we did when fat Marjorie's granddaughter went missing." Belinda and I had recently solved the case of the missing granddaughter…managing to draw the ire of a female agent with the Tennessee Bureau of Investigations at the same time.

"This *alleged* missing call girl situation isn't anything like Marjorie's case. You're connecting dots where there are none."

"I'm going to call that Papa Field's distribution place and see what I can find out about Scott Epperling."

"Oh, Leslie…let it go," she whined, but followed me into the kitchen. "What are you going to ask them?"

I found the number for the distribution center in Clifton and dialed. I kind of miss dialing. I always found the *schnickaty-schnickaty-schnick-schnick* sound very comforting. "I've got an idea."

"Oh man, let it go, and whatever you do, don't mention Lilly's missing call girl. Put it on speakerphone."

Grinning at my friend, I punched the button for the speakerphone. A lady answered almost immediately, and I ad-libbed, "Hello, my thirty-year-old son-in-law has recently been laid off from his job as a delivery truck driver. I just happened to stop by Sam Tackett's place the other day, and one of your delivery men came by—such a nice young man—I believe his name was Scott?"

"Yes, ma'am, that would have been Scott Epperling. What about Scott?"

"Oh, there wasn't the least little bitty thing wrong with Mr. Epperling. In fact, I was so impressed with his friendly and efficient manner that I wondered whether he wouldn't mind giving my son-in-law some pointers for when he goes out on interviews or whatever." I thought it sounded pretty lame, but the lady ate it up.

"Scott works the seven o'clock shift so he's normally back around four o'clock. If you wanted to have your son-in-law drop by around then, I'm sure Scott wouldn't mind talking to him. Scott's a good guy. He might even be able to steer your son-in-law to a job in the area."

"Do you know whether Mr. Epperling lives here in Clifton? If he has to commute to his job, I wouldn't want to make him late getting home to his family."

"Scott lives just a few blocks from our center. I doubt that it would be a problem at all. In fact, I'll mention to him that your son-in-law might be stopping by one afternoon. Scott won't mind at all."

I was smiling as I hung up the phone. I love Southern women. They love to help, and they love to talk about how much they love to help.

"Slick, Leslie, very slick. So, what good is this information?"

"I don't know... yet."

Chapter Five

Belinda made lunch at her place. She makes the best grilled-cheese sandwiches. She uses olive oil instead of butter. After finishing my sandwich, I took a sip of coffee. "That catsup lady told me Scott returns to the distribution center around four. Why don't we mosey on over there and follow Scott Epperling home?"

"Why on earth would we want to do that? Are you going to check his garage for bags of squirrels?"

"Maybe…if the opportunity presents itself."

Shaking her head, she said, "Nope…nope…nopey-nope…not going to happen."

"Okay, how about this. Big Lots is having a sale."

"Big Lots is always having a sale, Les. It's kind of what they do."

Next to Dollar General, Big Lots is my favorite store. They carry all sorts of discontinued stuff. I've gotten some great bargains at Big Lots. Unlike Dollar General, which has stuff piled on top of stuff, Big Lots store has stuff strewn all over the place—more like a warehouse than a store. It's fun to wander around in there.

"We can go over to Big Lots and then swing by the Papa Field's place afterward."

"Why?"

I flapped my arms, startling Riff, who had been sitting on my foot. "Sorry, Riff," I crooned. "Come here, baby."

Once settled in my lap, Riff gave a forgiving little sniff.

"You don't have to come if you don't want to. The Big Lots people don't fuss at me about carrying Riff around in the cart. We'll be okay without you."

"What are you going to do? I don't trust you."

"I thought maybe I could figure out where Papa Field lives. If I watched the house long enough, a family member might show up, and I could ask some questions about the virtual caravans of catsup running out to Tackett's place."

"Les, that is just ridiculous. If Papa Field was a Papa Field when he started the business back in the fifties, he'd be one hundred and twenty-years-old by now."

"The business is still in the family. Colonel Sanders didn't start Kentucky Fried Chicken when he was thirty years old. Did you ever see a picture of Colonel Sanders as a young man? No, you did not. He started out as old Colonel Sanders. He built up the business with his secret recipe and then left everything to the Sanders' clan. Papa Field must have done the same thing. Who knows what the family has had to do to stay in business. I mean, KFC has to compete with all kinds of other fast-food restaurants. KFC had to evolve to remain competitive."

"What does KFC have to do with this? They're still in chicken."

"Well, sure. But they had to get into baked, and grilled, and what have you. If we could talk with a member of the family—the dynasty, so to speak—perhaps we'd find out that Papa Field's is making something besides catsup."

"Like what?"

"Oh, I don't know! Hot sauce or something. Maybe something unrelated to a tomato-based compound?" I stuck a suspicious lilt to the question.

She rolled her eyes. "Here we go. Leslie, if the Papa Field's people are smuggling guns into Kentucky, they're not going to confess such an illicit activity to you. I see no value in accosting members of the Field family to determine why Sam Tackett is swimming in catsup."

She had made some valid points. I hate it when Belinda makes sense. "Fine."

"I can see you're going to pout until I give in. So fine, I'll tag along. We'll take the Riviera. If it starts to get dark, you can't see worth spit."

Again she was making sense. However, since I was getting three-quarters of what I had wanted in the first place, I let it ride.

• • •

I *yoo-hoo*ed through Belinda's front door at 2 P.M., carrying Riff and a plastic bag from Foodstuff City that held my stakeout gear (binoculars, night vision glasses, and a nifty pair of lighted reading glasses).

Belinda—dressed in jeans, a sweatshirt, and her walking shoes—greeted me with an "Uh-oh. You're dressed like Johnny Cash again."

I was wearing black pants, a black t-shirt with a skull on the front (a gift from my granddaughter a few years back), and Tom's old, black, lightweight jacket. I was also wearing my black Keds. I love Keds tennis shoes. I have them in a variety of tasteful colors.

"Hey, you're the one who said we might be out after dark. It never hurts to be prepared for every contingency. I see that you're also wearing dark clothing, so we are good to go."

Belinda climbed behind the wheel of the Riviera. I dragged the lead-filled passenger-side door open, fumbled with the seat latch, and deposited my grocery bag of gear and Riff in the backseat. I crawled into the seat and then stretched my body until I was able to haul the door closed with a vacuum-sucking *vwump*.

She grinned as I grappled with the shoulder harness. "I hate this big, stupid car."

"I know."

We goofed around at Big Lots until 3:30, then headed over to Papa

Field's distribution center. Belinda pulled into a parking lot off Main Street.

"This is an excellent location. Once Scott dumps his delivery truck for his personal vehicle, we can follow him, and the parking lot where the call girls saunter around is nearby on East Street. It's probably too early for them to be hanging around though."

"This is a dumb idea. I don't know why I always let you talk me into doing these fool things."

"Because you are my best friend in the entire world, and you don't have anything better to do."

"Oh yeah."

We chatted about nothing for a while until a Papa Field's delivery truck pulled into the distribution center lot across the street. "That's probably Scott."

"We don't know what his personal vehicle looks like. How am I supposed to know who to follow?"

"Wait for ten minutes and follow whatever pulls out onto Main."

Twenty minutes later a small, blue pickup pulled out onto the side street next to the distribution center and turned right at the stop sign on Main.

"Okay, Belinda, that's probably him. It's go time."

"Go time," she muttered, "this is dumb."

Pulling onto Main, we followed the blue truck through two lights. Belinda stayed with the truck and was doing very well, so I said, "You are doing very well, Belinda." We watched him pull into a driveway, park, and walk into a house. "That's definitely Scott Epperling. Pull up across the street but down a couple of houses."

We sat there for almost an hour without any activity. We were starting to get pretty bored. There is only so much nothing to talk about, even with your *best* friend. Suddenly a man's face filled Belinda's window.

We both yelled and jumped at the same time. It was a policeman. Belinda rolled down the window. "Oh, Officer, you scared us half to death," she said with a quiver in her voice.

"Is something wrong, ladies? We've received a couple of calls about a big, black car sitting here for close to an hour. What are you doing out here? It's starting to get dark." He narrowed his eyes and examined both of us. Riff was already trying to climb out the window in an attempt to reach the unexpected visitor, and Belinda caught her scrambling across the console from the backseat.

With sudden inspiration, I leaned over her to address the officer. "My friend here suspects her boyfriend is stepping out on her. We've been waiting here to see whether we can catch him in the act." I was proud of my on-the-spot creativity.

Belinda gave me her I-am-going-to-kill-you glare.

"Might as well admit it." I nodded at the officer helpfully. "It's the truth."

"Wait a minute," the officer said slowly. "Don't I know you, ladies?" I saw the recognition in his eyes. "Yeah, you're the two ladies from that cemetery thing, aren't you? Boy, that was quite a night." The officer was referring to the fat Marjorie case. He was still chuckling when I heard the slamming of a car door coming from the direction of Scott's house. Sure enough, his truck was backing onto the street.

I poked Belinda. "I don't think...um...Stanley is going anywhere tonight, Belinda." Directing a smile at the officer, I added, "Sorry if we annoyed the neighbors; we'll be moving along now if that's okay with you." Belinda switched on the ignition.

"Oh, sure." He straightened to his full height, still chuckling. "You ladies try to stay out of trouble." We smiled as we pulled away.

"I'm going to cut out your little, puny heart," Belinda growled.

"Pull into this driveway and turn around. The suspect's getting away."

She did as I directed but continued to spit venom at me. "How come it has to be me stalking some man like some kind of *Fatal Attraction* lunatic. How come you can't be the lunatic?"

"Because you're driving the car."

"What does that have to do with anything?"

"Because stalking lunatics are never the passengers, Belinda."

"In whose playbook?"

"I'm sorry, okay. I panicked. Did you see which way he turned? Boy, he was right. It is starting to get dark."

"I saw him. I'll follow him, but we are not finished with this discussion."

I wasn't worried. Belinda is my best friend in the whole world. She never stays mad at me for very long.

Ten minutes later she was still fuming. "You even called me by name!"

"So what, he already knows our names from the cemetery."

"Leslie Barrett, you will be the death of me. I swear! I'm going to have to move. I'm going to have to join the witness protection program. I'll become Juanita and move to Puerto Rico, somewhere you can never find me!"

"Oh, give it a rest, Juanita; you've had more fun since I came into your life, and you know it."

"You did not *come* into my life, Leslie. It's more like you barreled into it."

"Well, fine, call it whatever you want to. We still have a lot of fun. He's heading toward the Glen." I observed. It was past 8 P.M. and almost completely dark.

"Where are your night vision glasses?" I asked, twisting to grab my plastic gear bag.

"In the glove box," she directed. We had acquired two pairs of high-technology, high-definition night vision eyeglasses in preparation for a nighttime cemetery stakeout. They were a steal at Dollar General for $9.99 plus tax. Everything takes on an amber tint, and you can look straight at a flood light without any glare. Really cool. I got Belinda's glasses from the glove box and handed them over.

She adjusted them over her regular glasses. "Ooooooooooooo," we crooned in unison.

"He's turning," I said informatively.

"I can see that, Les."

"Well, yeah, *now* you can see him. Now that I gave you the night vision glasses."

"Harrumph," she harrumphed.

I noted the street name as we followed. "Prescott. Where does that go?"

"I'm not sure. A lot of the streets in the Glen weave all over the place."

"You know, Belinda, if you had a vehicle made in the twenty-first century, you'd have a navigation system."

"Your ice cream truck doesn't have a navigation system either, Leslie."

"I don't need one. My rearview mirror has that north-south-east-west feature."

She gave a theatrical wave at her rearview mirror. "My Riviera has the same feature. So, let's see"—she squinted at the mirror—"we are heading northeast, so, now that you have that invaluable information, where does Prescott go…huh?"

"Okay, fine…let's declare a truce. How about we figure out what Scott is up to first, and then we can fuss at each other. How's that?"

Before she could answer, Scott turned again. "Hang back, Belinda."

"I am hanging back," she grumbled, and slowly made the turn. We were now in a sparsely developed area. There are weird stretches throughout the Glen with several houses and then long gaps filled with wooded areas on both sides of the road. The Glen was all mapped out for future development, with grassy lanes carved out where streets would be one day. For now they just mow them once in a while. Scott's truck was turning down one of those lanes.

"Belinda," I whispered.

"I see him. What should we do?"

Belinda had been doing an excellent great job of hanging back, as I'd instructed. "Turn onto the lane just before the one he pulled down. When you turn though, go in dark."

She snorted. "Go in dark? I'm assuming you mean I should turn off the headlights?"

I snorted back at her, which caused her to laugh. She turned off the headlights as she was making the turn and whispered, "Officially going in dark, Chief."

Scott had not gone in dark. We could see his headlights bouncing deeper into the wooded area off to our right.

"I'm turning the lights on for a moment, Les. I don't want to run into a tree or anything."

"Okay, but shut them down once you have your bearings."

"Aye, aye, sir."

We laughed together at that. It was her way of letting me know that she was over her snit. Of course, it could come back later, but we were a team again…for now.

"It looks like he stopped."

"Going dark again," she muttered, crawling along the grassy lane parallel to where the truck sat with the headlights on. We were approximately two house lots away. Belinda squinted through the trees, mumbling, "What is he doing way out here in the middle of nowhere?"

The driver's-side door of the pickup truck opened, and the interior of the cab lit up briefly, followed by a soft slam of the door. We heard the crunch of footsteps, and Scott's silhouette was illuminated in his headlights as he trudged deeper into the woods.

"He's carrying something in each hand. I'm going to try to get close enough to see what he's up to," I whispered.

"I don't think it's a good idea for you to creep around out here like Rambo."

I harrumphed, and she added, "Wait…I'll turn off the interior light. Otherwise, we'll light up like a stadium when you open the door."

"Now you're thinking," I said appreciatively.

I quietly opened the passenger-side door and softly grunted as I levered my way out of the low-slung seat. "You keep Riff…," I started to whisper when there was a quick rustling in some leaves nearby, and Riff launched herself from the car, through the leaves, and into the darkness.

"Oh great," I mumbled. "Riff…come back here," I whispered into the darkness. When no Riff came snuffling from under the leaves, I started in after her.

"Leslie," Belinda hissed. I ignored her warning and, taking high steps to minimize the noise, entered the dark forest.

I high-stepped my way through the leaves, waving my arms in front of me like Frankenstein's monster. I was concentrating so hard on staying quiet that Belinda scared the crap out of me. I had only seconds of warning. I froze at the sounds of an animal's labored breathing coming from somewhere close by. Belinda walked right into me and nearly knocked me over.

"Holy crap, are you trying to kill me?"

"I came to save you."

"Thanks." I was glad to see her but didn't want her to know it. "Did Riff come back?"

"No…she's scuttling around out here somewhere."

We had managed to make our way about halfway through the trees to where Scott's truck was parked with headlights blazing. Fortunately,

I saw the tree before I slammed into it. "We'll wait behind this tree for a few minutes and see if he comes back."

"Okay. I guess it was a good thing we both wore dark clothing," she whispered just as a small, white, snuffling Riff came bounding through the leaves toward us, scaring the crap out of both of us.

I swept Riff into my arms, relieved at her safe return, and ready to scold her for the disappearing act, when brief flashes of bright light illuminated the woods.

"That's weird," I mumbled. "It looks like he's taking photographs or something."

We watched for about ten minutes, the three of us peering around the tree trunk. Suddenly, there was a crashing of furious activity coming from somewhere up ahead, beyond the reach of the truck's headlight beams.

"Oh my Lord!" Belinda's arms wrapped around me from behind. We heard a weird noise. Sort of a soft, echoing *thwip* and then again *thwip*. "What the heck was that?" she squeaked into my ear.

"Shhhhhh," I said as we stood glued to the tree, Belinda still hugging me tightly.

A bright light came on again in the woods and stayed on for a couple of minutes. We stood huddled together for several minutes in silence until we heard thumping and dragging sounds that made my teeth hurt. Loud human grunts accompanied the dragging sounds. I saw a humpbacked silhouette approaching the truck slowly through the headlight beams.

Thump…grunt…drag…thump…grunt…drag…a   gruesome, halting dance.

"Get down!" A whispered shriek tore through me like a living thing. I stuffed Riff and all her white fur inside Tom's black jacket as we dropped to the forest floor. "Cover your face."

We curled up like sow bugs, with the sleeves of our jackets slung across our faces. We lay there quaking…afraid to breathe. Even Riff was quiet, although she wriggled around inside my jacket until she finally managed to work her head out just below my chin. Belinda poked me with her finger to get my attention and nodded toward the source of the sounds.

Dust swirled in the headlight beams. I could clearly see a man straining to drag a non-moving, very heavy something. I stuffed a gasp down my throat. He was dragging what looked very much like a body clothed in dark material. He reached the front of the truck, then disappeared on the far side. The distinctive sound of a tailgate lowering squealed through the trees, followed by a long inhaled breath, a tremendous loud grunt, and the dull thud of a very unanimated something hitting the truck bed. We heard the tailgate lift and the *slikk* of its locking mechanism. We continued to watch as Scott returned to the dark woods, only this time we saw he was carrying a dim flashlight. We watched him disappear into the darkness and then reappear in the beams of the headlights. The truck's engine started, and the taillights lit up. Scott reversed his way down the lane to Prescott.

"Go…go…go," I urged Belinda as we creaked and staggered to our feet. We ran, Belinda in the lead in full Frankenstein-flailing form and me behind, one hand clutching Riff to my chest and a fistful of Belinda's jacket in the other. Neither of us cared any longer how much noise we were making. The hand of one of Belinda's antenna-like arms smacked against the Riviera, and she yelped. She hand-walked her way around the vehicle. I hauled open the passenger-side door, tossed in Riff, and scrabbled into the low seat. I huffed and groaned as I closed the heavy door. Both doors slammed in concert.

"Back up," I wheezed. "We need to see where he's going."

Seat belts clicked, the Riviera roared to life, headlights streamed through the trees. Belinda reversed swiftly, swinging out onto the paved street. She was marvelous. I swear, the way she was slinging that car around, she could be in an action-adventure movie. She slid the gearshift solidly into drive with an audible *thunk*, and we were off, gaining on Scott's taillights in the distance.

"*YA-HOO!*" I hollered at the top of my lungs.

Belinda replied with a maniacal laugh, and Riff barked excitedly from the backseat.

Scott Epperling drove home, pulling his truck into the garage.

"Well, that's it, Leslie. Let's go home."

I opened my mouth to argue, and she continued, "I know what you're going to say, and there's nothing to see in a dark garage!"

"Maybe he left the side door unlocked. One time our smoke alarm went off, and the alarm-monitoring people called me. I rushed home to find that the stupid fire department people had busted through the garage door. Sheesh, the side door was unlocked. They didn't even try it. They just got a battering ram and ruined the garage door. It turned out that nothing was on fire anyway. We never did figure out why the smoke alarm went off."

"That's all very interesting. What does it have to do with tonight?"

"The side door to Scott's garage could be unlocked." I grabbed my plastic gear bag and held up my nifty pair of lighted reading glasses. "Here, I brought my reading glasses with the headlights. If the door is unlocked, I can find out what he has rolled up in that tarp. If the door is locked, I'll look through the window."

I put on the reading glasses and flipped the switches. These things are a swell combination of reading glasses with twin beams of light.

Belinda had cruised past Scott's house by this time and was looping around the block to head back to Main Street. Glancing over, she let loose a snorting laugh. "Where in the heck did you get those? You look like one of the mole people!"

"Pull down Scott's street. It won't hurt anything for me to look."

Turning off Main again and onto Scott's street, Belinda chuckled. "Seriously, Les, did you get those glasses at Dollar General or Big Lots?"

"Neither…I saw them in a catalog for twenty dollars. Originally, they were created for people who want to read in bed without disturbing their bedmate, but I keep mine beside the bed in case there's a blackout."

"I have a regular old flashlight beside the bed that runs on boring old D batteries that works just fine in a blackout. What do those things take?"

"Watch batteries. The batteries came with the glasses. I think they're great. You know how blind I am at night."

"Leslie, you have nightlights everywhere. Mice could land airplanes in your hallway."

I like my nifty glasses, and I fully intended to use them. We were cruising in front of Scott's house. "Pull up across the street."

"Les, I admit I want to know what is in that tarp. Assuming you discover it's a deceased human, anything you find will be thrown out in court. Face it, you have no legal right to enter that garage and search that man's truck."

"I don't care. I have to try. I hate it when you spout legal stuff at me. You and I both know there aren't two hundred squirrels rolled up in that tarp. He wasn't out there long enough to herd two hundred squirrels into a body bag. There also weren't any call girls roaming around in those woods. He killed one of our deer. That's it flat-out; that's it."

Reluctantly my best friend parked across from Scott's and turned off the headlights. With a weary sigh she admitted, "I think you're right. Just don't do anything dumb. Verify there's a deer in the bed of that truck and then we call 911. That's all."

"Agreed. Oh…is the interior light still off?" I whispered.

"Yes…but that isn't going to make a hell of a lot of difference unless you turn off those skinny beams of light on your reading glasses. Why do you need reading glasses? Take the flashlight."

I switched off the glasses and climbed out, muttering, "These glasses are awesome."

I was careful not to let Riff escape and disappear into the dark again. I quietly *snikked* the door closed. Once my eyes were as adjusted to the dark as they were going to get, I set off across the street, up Scott's driveway, and around the side of the garage. Scott didn't have any outside lights on at all. If I was into whatever Scott is into, I wouldn't make it easy for investigators either.

I turned the doorknob on the side door to the garage and found it was locked. I plastered my face against the window part of the door and switched on the high beams. I couldn't see a thing…I mean nothing, nada, zilch. I had blinded myself with the reflected light. I'm going to post a warning online.

I blinked away the echoing orbs of light. It took a few minutes for my retinas to recover. When I could see well enough to pick my way back across the street, I rounded the Riviera and slid into the passenger seat without comment.

"Well, did you see anything?"

I didn't feel it was necessary to educate my friend about what happens when one fries one's retinas with nifty lighted reading glasses, so I simply admitted, "No, the door was locked. I couldn't see a thing. I know there's a dead Glen deer in that pickup. I'm pretty sure that was a rifle he was carrying when he got back to the truck."

"Les, we should go home now."

"It is a deer…isn't it?"

When we reached the stop sign, my friend looked at me and sighed before pulling onto Main Street. "I really…really…*really* hate to admit it when you're right. However, I can't think of anything else that it could be except deer poaching. It did look as though he was carrying a rifle."

"There weren't any shots. Maybe he used a silencer, and that was what that *thwip* noise was. As long as we're out this late, drive by that parking lot where Mrs. Towers claims the call girls hang out. It's over there across from Papa Field's."

"No…I'm done. We're going home. I'm not the least bit interested in picking up a call girl. Besides, that place is over near Papa Field's and Big Lots, and we were just there."

"Those women don't come out until after dark. It's after dark. Mrs. Towers is expecting us to look into that girl's disappearance."

"You aren't trying to conflate whatever is going on with Scott and Sam with Lilly's missing call girl, are you? If Scott is carting call girls out there along with deer, there wouldn't be much room left in that truck for catsup. What's your plan, Les? Are you going to count the women to determine whether anyone is missing? It won't do you any good to count them. You don't know the original inventory. How are you going to know whether someone is missing?"

"Just drive by. That's all I'm suggesting. Just drive by, and then we will go home. I promised Mrs. Towers."

She mumbled, "I don't know why I go along with you on these wild hairbrained ideas of yours." Belinda worked her way around behind the catsup distribution center and onto East Street. As we got closer to the parking lot, I told her to slow down. In the shadow of a streetlight, I saw a large woman leaning against a car in the infamous parking lot.

"Pull over to the curb here," I directed.

"Why? You said we were going to drive by."

"Just pull over and turn off the lights."

With a groan, she did as I asked, and I hit the automatic window thing to roll down my window.

"Oh man, now what are you doing?" She sighed.

"*Yoo-hoo!*" I hollered, waving at the large woman.

"Are you out of your mind? We've already been stopped by the police once tonight. You're going to get us arrested for solicitation."

"We are not soliciting. The call girls are soliciting. We are just a couple of nice, old ladies asking for directions."

The woman to whom I had *yoo-hoo*ed was approaching at a wary pace. When she got closer to the car, Riff stuck her head up and placed two paws on the window sill, panting happily, with her tail wagging in greeting.

The woman lost all fear and scooted right up beside the car. "Well, hello there, cutie," she greeted Riff, and gave her a scratch behind the ear. She took a step back from the car and smiled a question at me. "What choo ladies doing out here?" She was a large girl, stuffed into a skirt with mounded boobs spilling from her blouse. I looked at her feet and was surprised to see she wore sneakers. Noting the direction of my eyes, the woman deadpanned, "Can't run in high heels."

"Aren't you freezing, honey?" I asked, pulling Riff back and depositing her in the back.

"Nah…I'm hot-blooded. You two ladies out slumming?"

"No, I just wanted to know whether any of your…um…colleagues have gone missing lately."

"Leslie, don't be ridiculous." I could hear the embarrassed cringe in her voice.

The young woman stared at me with a Mona Lisa smile until I finally understood. "Oh yeah," I pawed through my purse and came up with a twenty-dollar bill. I had barely raised it to the window when it evaporated into thin air like a magic trick.

Belinda groaned, "Oh no…"

"Shhhhhh, Belinda."

I asked the woman again. "So, are any of your…um…friends… missing?"

The woman replied with a scrunched-up expression that suggested deep thought, "Wouldn't 'xactly say she was missing, but I haven't seen Kiki lately."

"Kiki? Is that her real name?"

She snorted. "I kinda doubt it. Why? You looking for Kiki?"

"Not exactly…how old is Kiki? What does she look like?"

She frowned, then gave a what-the-heck shrug. "It's hard to guess… late teens or early twenties…blond." She laugh-snorted again. "She claims she's a natural blond…but, trust me, you can't blame God for *that* color!"

"Is she skinny or fat? What's her last name?"

She shrugged again. "Even if I knew Kiki's real name, I wouldn't give it to you. She's skinny. A lot of the girls are skinny." She huffed up proudly and thrust her boobs even higher. "You know, some men like a woman with some meat on her bones. I get the meat lovers."

Belinda gave an agonizing mewl and whispered, "Finish up, Les. I'm driving away."

I flapped my hand at her dismissively and continued the conversation. "How long ago did Kiki disappear?"

"I never said she disappeared, lady. I said I haven't seen her around. These are funny questions. What's going on? Has something happened to Kiki?"

Belinda leaned her long body in front of mine and spoke toward the passenger-side window, "Kiki is probably fine. My friend is just nosy. Nice talking to you. We're leaving now."

"Thank you, miss." I hesitated. "What's your name again?"

With a big grin and a toss of her hair, she laughed. "Anything you want it to be, sugar."

Belinda harrumphed and returned to her driving position.

"Okay...well, thank you. If Kiki doesn't show up soon, you may want to file a missing person's report."

"Yeah, right...like I'm going to call the po-leece. What am I supposed to tell them? I want to report a missing hooker...goes by the name of Kiki...god-awful blond hair, and chicken scrawny. Yeah, lady, the po-leece gonna jump right on that one."

I had a great idea. "Hey, I've got a great idea. If you aren't comfortable going to the police, let the lady in that beauty shop over there know that Kiki is missing." I pointed in the direction of Lilly's shop and opened the passenger-side door. "Let me show you."

Belinda growled, "Leslie Barrett, do not get out of this car."

Grabbing the red plastic handle of Riff's leash from beside my feet, I held it up. "No worries, I'll take Riff."

Hearing her name, Riff yipped excitedly. I clipped the leash to her collar and pushed the heavy door open with a grunt.

"Leslie, seriously, do *not* get out of this car."

The call girl aided me by hauling the door all the way open. Those big doors hang out like Dumbo's ears. I swear that sucker can probably fly. "Thank you so much." Riff in my arms, I groaned my way from the car, silently commending my best friend for having left the interior light off. Dropping Riff to the sidewalk, I shoved the heavy door closed, being careful not to make a racket. It still went *thud!*

Belinda called through the open window in a low grumble, "Don't get into trouble." Then the window zipped up, and I heard the *thunk* of the car's door locks. I started off down the sidewalk, with Riff dancing alongside. The call girl stared at me. "Well, c'mon; I'll show you where Lilly's place is. By the way, my name is Leslie."

With a shrug she followed. "Joy Mountain," she said.

"Come again?"

"My name. Not my real name. My…"

"Professional name?" I suggested.

She threw a broad grin my way. "Exactly!"

"Pleased to meet you, Joy." I linked my arm with hers and whispered, "If anybody approaches us, you are taking your grandma, and her puppy, for a walk."

We sauntered down the sidewalk with Riff drifting back and forth. We walked about half a block. I stopped to point across the street into the dark. "You can't see her shop right now, it's too dark, but it's right over there near the parking lot for the catsup place. You can go right in there and tell Lilly you're worried about your friend. She'll contact the police. That will keep you out of it but still have somebody looking for your friend."

"Leslie…you're the one claiming Kiki is missing. Why don't *you* call the po-leece? And, Kiki ain't my friend."

"Well, colleague then. Hey, Joy, do you know anybody over there at Papa Field's Catsup? Do they ever work at night?" The parking lot at Papa Field's was dimly lit.

"Why you askin' about the catsup place?"

"No reason. I just wondered. So, do you ever see anybody over there at night?"

Joy huffed impatiently. "There's usually one fella over there until around nine. Nobody there this late. It's not always the same fella cleaning the delivery vans, and no, we didn't proposition him."

I offered a look of incredulity. "Of course you don't. That would be rude and unprofessional."

"Dang right." She huffed.

"So, this guy cleans out the delivery vans? What does he do?"

"I don't make a habit of staring at the clean-up guy. There's one guy that really gets into it though."

"What do you mean?"

"Most of the guys wash and hose down the outside of the delivery trucks, but there's one guy who goes to town hosing out the inside of trucks and everything."

That piqued my interest. "All the trucks, or just one of them?"

"How should I know? I just noticed is all, in between…uh…my clients."

Riff was ready to go home. She was pawing at my feet. Lights flashed from behind us. I turned to see Belinda turning the headlights on and off. "Joy, looks like one of your *clients* is trying to get your attention."

She shook her head. "Nuh-uh…that's your friend. She's been crawling behind us the whole time."

The passenger-side window whizzed down, and I heard the *thunk* of the doors unlocking. "Leslie," my friend's voice carried through the window.

"Better go now. Nice to have met you, Miss Mountain. If Kiki doesn't turn up soon, go on in and tell Lilly."

Joy grinned and watched as I swung the big door open and Riff jumped inside. I lowered myself into the low-slung seat, and Joy shoved the steel trap closed. I turned to speak to Joy through the window but never got the chance.

Belinda hollered, "Bye," and practically took my nose off when the window slapped shut, effectively cutting off any further conversation.

"Hey," I complained. Belinda ignored me, turned on the headlights, and away we went.

We were already on Trendle Road, heading back to the Glen. "What a nice lady. Her professional name is Joy Mountain."

Belinda gave an unladylike snort. "Joy Mountain?"

"Yeah…so? What's wrong with you?"

"What's wrong with *me*? What's wrong with *you*? Hopping out of the car? You always get in trouble when you leave the car."

"I learned a lot of useful information." I filled her in on what Miss Mountain had to say about the fellas over at the catsup place.

"So what? It makes sense for somebody to wash the trucks at night." Curious now, she asked, "She didn't say anything about that Scott guy?"

"No." My voice trembled. "I know he's killing our deer. What are we going to do?"

"We will call Chief Braddock and report our suspicions…and don't you dare mention anything to him about missing prostitutes."

"*Call girls*, Belinda. Not prostitutes. Sheesh! Mrs. Towers has got me so well trained I'll probably never use the words *prostitute* or *hooker* again." Riff plopped onto my lap like a ten-pound ham. "Riff, you're definitely going on a diet."

Happy to be included in the conversation, Riff panted a smile my way and resettled. "There isn't anything Quinn can do. After listening to you for the last five years, I've picked up some legal stuff of my own. Quinn won't have justifiable means to get a judge to sign a search warrant. We're just those two loony ladies who keep getting mixed up in stuff. Nobody is going to listen to us. We need proof, and the only way to get it is to find out what Scott has rolled up in that tarp. I'll bet you a hundred dollars that he totes that horrid bundle out to Sam Tackett's place in the morning so Sam can cut up one of our deer into pork chops…or deer chops or whatever. I know you don't think there's a connection to Kiki's disappearance, but if you think outside of the box, who knows?" I shrugged dramaticly. "Scott and Sam could be running a…um…call girl service operation out there as well as poaching deer. It can't be a coincidence that the call girls are right there across the street from Papa Field's and *poof*, Kiki goes missing. Hunters probably get lonely for female companionship."

"Les, hunters are weekend warriors. They aren't stranded on a battle-field in France fighting the Nazis."

We were back on Trendle, heading toward the Glen. "Keep going, Belinda. Let's check out Tackett's for a little look-see."

"At what? It's already pitch-dark. The place is closed."

"Then there's no risk in driving out there, is there?"

"You are infuriating! If I drive out there, will you shut up and then we go home? No stopping? No getting out of the car?"

"Yes."

True to her word, she cruised out Trendle Road. We crossed the bridge at Mogey Creek. "Tackett's place is just ahead. Pull into the parking lot."

"Oh no. That wasn't part of this deal. You said you would shut up and go home if I drove us out here. I've kept my part of the bargain."

"We have to turn around somewhere. Might as well turn around at Tackett's."

She made a big deal out of smacking the turn signal on to make the left into the front lot. "Pull around back," I instructed.

"Leslie…"

"Big deal. So we cruise around the building before heading back to the Glen. Just do it."

She did it. "I'm surprised he doesn't have security lights out here," she muttered. "That's strange. Why have an elaborate inside security system and totally ignore the outside perimeter?"

I had her hooked. "That's a good question and an astute observation, Belinda."

"Flattery isn't going to work."

We rounded the side of the building. "Don't even think about it, Leslie. I'm not bouncing down that dirt track on past that prefab building in search of tarp bundles."

The headlights swept the area. I waited until we were alongside the back door until hollering for her to stop. "*STOP!*"

I yelled loud enough that she slammed her foot on the brake in surprise. "What? What?"

"Put the car in park. I want to check something."

"You are *not* getting out of this car," she growled, allowing the car to roll forward.

"Come on; we've come this far."

Blowing an exasperated breath, she braked again and slid the gearshift forward. "You've got three minutes. Three minutes and I'm leaving."

I shoved Riff into her arms, plowed my way out of the tank, and pushed the door closed as quietly as possible. I approached the door beside the loading dock. The Riviera's headlights provided the only light. I walked the few steps back to the driver's-side window. The window slid down. "What?"

"Hand me the flashlight."

"No. Get back in the car."

I gave my best friend my most serious glare. "Fine," she huffed, rustled around in the plastic sack, and handed over the heavy flashlight.

Without comment, I returned to the exit door. Playing the flashlight beam on the doorknob, I turned the knob.

Nothing.

I heard Belinda growling. "What are you doing? Of course the door is locked. There isn't anything to see."

I ignored her, trotted up the steps leading to the loading dock, and approached the garage-style door. It had one of those crank handles on it. Placing the flashlight at my feet, I put my back against the door and grasped the handle with both hands. Remembering to lift with my knees, I yanked the handle.

Nothing.

I learned from my mother that if you yank hard enough and long enough on a mechanism, the mechanism will eventually give way. So I took a deep breath and bobbed up and down in a furious attempt to jar the door open. It worked, sort of.

A high-pitched sound echoed within the building. *EEEEEEEEE EEEEEEEEE EEEEEEEEE.*

Abandoning my efforts at clandestine breaking and entering, I swept the flashlight into my hand, bounded down the steps, and raced around the front of the Riviera. My butt had barely landed on the seat when I got a face full of fur. My best friend tore out of there like Smokey and the Bandit. I was juggling Riff and fumbling for the seat belt. Fully expecting the front lot to be swarming with patrol cars and good-ole-boy pickups at the sound of the alarm, there was nothing but an empty front lot. Belinda immediately peeled out onto Trendle and was across the Mogey Creek bridge in seconds.

"Perfect Polly," I asked.

"Had to be. You yanking up and down on that door caused enough vibration to set off the internal alarm."

"Slow down! We don't want to look suspicious when the police head out this way."

"I'm slowing down." She did but made a prediction. "I don't think there will be any police cars. Why weren't any outside alarms going off? Nobody is inside that building this late at night. What good is an internal alarm? My guess is, Tackett has his security system set to alert him at home somehow."

"What's to say it doesn't also alert the police?"

"If he wanted to alert the cops, why wouldn't there be an outside alarm whooping it up back there?" She shook her head. "Sam Tackett wants to be alerted, but he doesn't want the authorities roaring out here, Leslie. As much as I hate to admit it, there is definitely something fishy going on between Scott Epperling and Sam Tackett."

I sat back in the seat with satisfaction, hugging my ball of fur to my chest.

Chapter Six

It was close to 10 P.M. when we pulled into Belinda's garage. She climbed out and started up the step to enter the house when she realized I hadn't gotten out of the car.

She walked back and opened the passenger-side door. "Why are you still sitting there?"

"I can't move. I'm pretty sure I've strained every muscle in my body. Are there muscles in your ears? Even my ears hurt."

Chuckling, she helped me out of the low-slung seat, and I shuffled behind my friend to the door, with Riff draped over one arm.

Once we were inside, I dropped Riff a few inches from the floor, and she immediately sought out Butter's water dish. "Want a Diet Coke?" Belinda was already rooting around in the refrigerator.

I accepted the cold bottle. "We've come a long way tonight. We're in agreement that something very hinky is going down and that it has something to do with the deer in the Glen. What do you think made that *thwip* noise?"

"I have no idea what a gunshot sounds like—silenced or not—other than what you hear on TV and in the movies. It was an odd sound. A regular gunshot would have been loud and likely would have carried an echo. Even one of those Burt Reynolds' crossbows would have a more lethal sound. *Thwip...thwip...*doesn't sound like much."

"Whatever he used brought down something of good size. These creeps are rustling our deer, Belinda. What are we going to do about it? Even if we call him, Quinn isn't going to do anything, and he most definitely isn't going to see the link to Kiki."

"There is no link to Kiki. Kiki is an entirely unrelated issue, assuming there even *is* a Kiki issue."

"You heard Joy Mountain. Kiki is missing."

"You've got to stop plucking jigsaw pieces out of thin air and jamming them into some bizarre puzzle of your own making!"

"That sounded kind of profound."

"Okay, we agree that something is going on, and we agree it has something to do with the deer in the Glen. Unfortunately, we also agree that calling the police will likely prove to be fruitless."

Riff was sitting on my foot, and I gathered her up and into my lap. "We have to follow through on all this. You know how I feel about coincidences. Our deer are being *thwip*ped, Kiki the *call girl* is missing, and something big is going on out there at Sam Tackett's place. I mean, how much catsup does one store need? What are we going to do?"

"We follow Scott Epperling again and see whether he goes back out to Sam's place in the morning. I know I'm not normally the one to suggest such a thing, but I don't see any other way to find out whether Scott and Sam are tied together in the *thwip* mystery."

"In the morning? Scott starts his shift at seven o'clock. I won't be conscious that early. Why don't we go back to Scott's place, bust into his garage, peek under the blue tarp to verify a dead deer, and put a tracking device on the truck."

"We don't have a tracking device."

"The Dollar General is still open. We can run up there and get one."

"Let me get this straight." This was her Belinda-talking-to-a-moron voice. "If we drive back out to Scott's place, break down the door, verify that he has a dead deer in the bed of the truck...or...in your wildest hairbrained fantasies...Kiki, the dead *call girl*, we won't be able to call

911 because everything we discover will be thrown out in court."

"Oh, stop playing Ben Matlock. If there's a dead Kiki underneath that blue tarp, you'll never get me to believe that Scott Epperling won't end up doing some serious time in the pokey!"

"I'm betting it's a deer. Calling 911 to report a dead deer in the back of a guy's truck, parked in said guy's garage, isn't going to mobilize the National Guard. We would still need to follow this fabulous nine-dollars-and-ninety-nine-cents As Seen On TV tracking device out to Sam Tackett's place in the morning. Then what? We still can't involve the authorities because we don't have any proof that crimes are being committed. Whatever we end up doing is going to involve tomorrow morning."

Even though I knew I would be a total wreck at that time of the morning, I couldn't come up with a better plan. Something had to be done, and it was up to us to do it. We decided Belinda would be at my place at six o'clock to roust Riff and me from bed. We would take my Soul on the off chance Scott had noticed the Riviera.

Riff and I went home. I washed my face, brushed my teeth, and crawled into bed, with Riff curled at my side. It had been a long day. Instead of sugar plums, sex slavery and deer assassinations danced in my head. There was no way I was going to sleep. I closed my eyes, sighed mightily, and immediately went to sleep.

Chapter Seven

At 6:00 A.M. Belinda was lying on the doorbell. She has a key, but I got the point. I didn't bother going to the front door but rather staggered into the bathroom. I could hear her bumping around in the kitchen and talking with Riff-Raff. I turned on the shower and stood under the spray for several minutes. I made no attempt to wash anything. I merely blinked up into the water to nudge my brain toward consciousness. I towel dried my hair and just let it go. I have some unfortunate natural curl to my hair. Unless I blow-dry it into my usual sleek Doris Day–like bob, my hair dries in limp linguini curls.

I quickly dressed while I blessed and cursed Belinda. Blessed, because she had made coffee and filled my pump-thermos. Cursed, because she was the reason I was up at this ungodly hour.

Setting her empty coffee cup on the counter, she announced, "I took Riff out to potty, so we're ready to go."

"I'm not ready yet," I grumbled. Morning people are very irritating.

I bumbled around the kitchen and ate a granola bar. Belinda became impatient and herded me toward the garage. She poured me and my thermos of coffee into the passenger seat and announced, "I'm driving."

She slammed the door on me. I grumbled, "Damn right you're driving. This whole thing was your idea."

She opened the driver's-side door, reached in, and pushed the mechanism that releases the seat and slid it as far back as it would go.

Climbing in, I watched as she fiddled with the rearview mirror and both side mirrors until she adjusted them to her satisfaction. Finally, she started the car. Riff was asleep in the backseat on her blanket with her head tucked under her tail, her version of a sleep mask. Belinda punched the garage door opener clipped to the passenger-side visor and backed out of the garage.

"It's going to take me forever to get everything reset, you know. I had everything exactly as I like it. Now I'm going to have to start all over again." I sounded like a four-year-old. I didn't care. Have I mentioned that I hate mornings?

I pumped a mug of coffee from the thermos at my feet. As I was busy sulking, I didn't offer any to Belinda. By the time we got to Clifton, I was starting to engage in the day and offered my friend a pumped mug of coffee.

"No thanks, I had two cups while I was waiting for you."

Belinda turned down Scott's street. "What are you doing? I thought we were going to follow Scott from the catsup place."

"Leslie, Scott has that tarp-covered thing in his personal truck, not the catsup truck."

"Oh yeah, I forgot."

"You forgot? Wake up! You're the one who started this whole thing."

"I know…I know…but you agreed something weird is going on. You know how much I hate mornings. Riff and I got up at the *crap of dawn* as you requested… doesn't mean I have to be all perky or anything," I finished with a grumble.

I thought of something and swore, "Crap, I forgot my stakeout bag."

"Your Foodstuff City bag is in the back. I transferred it from the Riviera to your Soul."

Unclipping my seat belt, I twisted to kneel on the seat and reached into the back. "I'm glad one of us can think at predawn."

I settled back in my seat and inventoried the contents of my plastic sack: flashlight (check), night vision glasses (check), binoculars (check), reading glasses with tiny headlights (check). I mumbled, "I could probably get by without the flashlight."

"Refasten your seat belt. What are you looking for?"

I high-handed the binoculars, then looked around for a couple of seconds. "Pull straight into that driveway directly across from Scott's. Don't pull all the way in next to the house, just leave the back end of the Soul flush with the street."

She did as I suggested and switched off the ignition. I twisted around again to kneel in the passenger seat, training the binoculars through the rear hatch window. The Kia Soul has tremendous visibility. Playing around with the focus knobs, I muttered, "This is no good. All I can see is the front of the garage."

"Settle down, Les; there isn't anything to see yet. Wait until he backs out of the garage. I don't know what you hope to see anyway. We already know he has that blue bundle in the bed of the truck. We're here to see where he goes with it."

I stayed in place until my legs started to cramp. Of course, the minute I swiveled back around into the seat, Belinda hollered, "The garage door is going up!"

I crimped my way back into binocular position and focused on the rear of Scott's truck.

"Do you see anything?"

"Just a second…he's getting out of the cab, walking around the truck, lowering the lift gate. Oh. My. God."

"What's wrong? What is it?"

I continued to watch for a few seconds, lowered the binoculars, and looked into the eyes of my best friend. "It moved. Whatever he has in the back of that truck, it just moved."

While we sat in the driveway across from the Epperling residence, I kept up a running dialogue with Belinda as to what I saw with the aid of the binoculars. I described the twitching blue tarp. Then Scott crawled up into the truck bed and fiddled with something. I continued to watch, but after one more twitch, there was no further movement.

• • •

Scott pulled out of his driveway.

"Don't follow him too closely."

Scott turned down a side street that ran alongside the distribution center, passing the center and pulling his small truck into the call girls' parking lot directly across the street. Belinda followed and continued past the lot. I lowered the passenger-side window and stuck my head out to look behind us. I ducked my head back inside the car, holding tight to the squirming Riff. An open car window is too much temptation for Riff to pass up. "Belinda, he ran across the street toward the distribution center."

"What is he up to?"

"Turn into Lilly's place. Let's just sit there for a few minutes and see what happens."

"What is he up to?" Belinda muttered again as she swung into one of Lilly's parking spaces.

Ten minutes passed. Finally, our wait paid off as a Papa Field's Catsup delivery truck exited the distribution center and then zipped into the call girls' lot, where he had left his truck. "Of course! Les, don't you see? He couldn't make the transfer at the distribution center without all holy hell breaking out."

Scott hopped from the delivery truck, went around to the back, and opened the back double-hung doors. He walked over to his little blue truck and lowered the lift gate. We watched as he backed the delivery truck as close as possible to the blue truck, practically kissing it in the process. It didn't take long for him to slide the blue-tarp-covered bundle from the bed of his truck and up into the back of the delivery truck. Then he reversed his movements with the lift gate and the rear doors of the delivery truck before climbing behind the wheel.

"You're supposed to stay at least three cars behind the person you're following," I cautioned as she pulled into the side street to follow.

"Yeah, well, I'm not sitting here waiting for three cars to wander past us. He could be halfway to Nashville by that time."

"Okay, but try to hang back a little."

She pulled up to the stop sign, preparing to make the turn back onto Main Street. "Hurry up or we're going to lose him."

"Make up your mind, Les. Hang back or hurry up?"

Belinda had been careful to allow a couple of vehicles get between us and Scott, but we were now well beyond the Glen and heading north on Trendle Road. The farther north we traveled, the less traffic we encountered until it was just us and Scott. She was practically riding the brake pedal to let Scott drift ahead of us.

"He's going to Tackett's."

"It looks that way. There isn't much else out this way."

"Maybe it's still alive. Whatever he has in that truck, let's pray we're not too late."

Tears leaked from her eyes. "I should have allowed you to do your breaking-and-entering routine last night. That poor animal must have been in agony all night." She slapped the steering wheel with both hands vehemently. "What kind of creep doesn't put a wounded animal out of its misery?"

"He's just a catsup truck driver, Belinda, not a master hunter or anything. He probably thought it was dead."

"I swear, if that jerk killed Jane Doe, I'm going to hang *him* upside down in the reindeer playroom!"

Belinda was poking along way behind the delivery truck when, sure enough, we watched Scott turn in at Sam Tackett's place.

"He'll probably pull around back, so give him a couple of minutes before we follow him. Maybe hang out on the side of the building. I'll get out and watch from around the corner to see what he's doing. When the coast is clear, I'll motion you forward and then you can pull around back."

She whispered urgently, "Here we go again. Do not get out of the car. Let's call Quinn now."

I waved my hand at her in a *pooh-pooh*ing motion. Belinda rolled up next to the building. I gave Riff to her and eased open my car door. Riff whined her frustration at not being allowed to follow—the little dickens likes to be in on the action. I pushed the car door almost closed. Moving with caution, I congratulated myself on my Keds tennis shoes and their rubber-soled bottoms. There was only the slightest sound of shifting gravel as I crept to peer around the corner. Scott was parked a few feet from the building. I watched as he climbed from the cab and walked confidently to the back entrance of Tackett's establishment. As soon as the door closed behind him, I crept around the corner. Seconds later, the back door flew open again. I executed a line-dancing maneuver referred to as a jazz box to reverse course and slip back around to the side of the building.

When she saw me, Riff started barking. I threw my stricken look toward Belinda. She had Riff in a headlock. I peeked around the corner again. Scott must have heard the commotion, because he was walking toward me with a look of curiosity on his face.

I started racing down the side of the building toward the front. Belinda had gotten the message. She kept pace with me, and we turned the corner almost in unison. I'm amazed she can drive as well in reverse as she can going forward. She should be in the movies. I flattened my back against the wood front of Tackett's bait shop. Belinda had whipped around the corner in reverse and stared at me through the open window, Riff's white head poking up over the top edge. Finger to my lips, I cautioned Riff to shush. If Scott came around this corner now, I would have to spin some kind of story. I wasn't running anymore.

We waited. Nothing happened. Belinda pointed at me and held up her palm in a gesture to stay there. I stayed, and she rolled forward to turn the corner. Smart woman. A car turning the corner wouldn't look suspicious. A blond-haired hobbit hugging the wall like Spider Man, however, might seem just a tad curious. I peered around the corner and watched her crawl forward. With the nose of the Soul poking around the back corner, she waved her arm through the open window, giving me the all clear.

I love that woman.

I walked swiftly along the building. Turning the corner, I abandoned caution and raced across the back lot directly toward the rear of the delivery truck. Belinda zoomed up beside the truck and angle-parked directly in front of it, effectively blocking any chance of escape.

I was already jerking on the handles at the back of the delivery truck to open the doors when she joined me. I hauled one door as she yanked the other one open, and together we folded both of them back. Riff was hopping around at our feet, then suddenly darted off down the dirt track and past the prefab barn-like structure.

I opened my mouth to holler at her when Belinda whispered, "Let her go, Les. Call 911; I'm going to check on the status of our patient."

She nimbly climbed into the recesses of the truck, and I followed, a little less nimbly, punching 911 into my cell phone.

When the 911 lady answered, I yelped, "Help! Send the police, send whoever can get here. We are at Sam Tackett's place on Trendle Road just north of Fairlawn Glen."

In a practiced and almost robotic voice, the lady asked, "What is the nature of your emergency?"

"I don't know yet," I answered. Belinda was talking to the lump beneath the blue tarp."

I pointed at the floor. "Look at these stains, Belinda. That looks like blood."

The 911 lady no longer sounded bored. "What did you say, ma'am? Is somebody injured? Ma'am, you need to give me more information."

Belinda wrestled with the blue tarp, "Help me with this, Leslie."

I barked into the phone, "Just send help, lady! *Now!*" Without disconnecting, I jammed the still-squawking phone into my pocket.

I took two steps toward Belinda but was interrupted by Scott Epperling's yell. *"Hey, what's going on out here. Get out of my truck!"*

Scott had exited the building and was heading toward the truck. I quickly surveyed the area in search of a weapon. All I saw was catsup. I grabbed two bottles from a nearby case and heaved them at Scott. One went skidding across the pavement, but the bottom of the second missile landed on the pavement with a loud *blop* right in front of Scott. Catsup spurted from the bottle, and Scott danced away from the carnage. I threw another bottle and then another, all the while screaming, *"You are a monster! Take that (throw) and that."* The next bottle socked him smack in the chest. Geysers of catsup were exploding everywhere.

"OW…stop that! What the hell…" He batted away another missile.

Dang plastic bottles nowadays.

Riff reappeared, yipping and yapping at Scott's feet, causing him to hop and whirl around. She was a little yip-yapping rocket.

I stopped heaving bottles because I was afraid I'd hit Riff. I was determining my next move when Belinda yelled, "It's alive; it's a deer!"

I screamed at Scott Epperling, "You've been stealing our deer! I already called the police! You may as well give up, you...you creep!"

Riff was doing an excellent job running circles around Scott like a maniac, so I crept two steps closer to where Belinda sat with the head of a good-size deer in her lap.

She held up a syringe with a yellow push-plunger thing on the end of a wicked dart. "Les, this deer has been drugged."

"Hey, lady, call off this fur ball!" Scott yelled.

Sam burst through the back door demanding, *"What in tarnation is going on out here?"*

If I had any measure of cool left, I lost it then. Snatching the yellow-knobbed syringe from Belinda's hand, I ran back to the truck and shook it furiously at Scott. *"You drugged a deer? You kidnapped and drugged one of our deer? Who in the blazes do you think you are?"*

I directed my next slur toward Sam. "And you! Scott kidnaps our deer, then you carve them into little four-pound roasts! You both make me sick!"

With the 911 lady squawking in one pocket, I jammed the poison-laced dart into my free pocket as evidence. I grabbed two more bottles of catsup and hollered at Riff, "Get over here! Get out of the way!" She immediately broke off her barking tirade and ran toward the back of the delivery truck.

As soon as Riff was safely out of range, I heaved both bottles of catsup at the men.

Scott and Sam hopscotched their way around red smears of catsup trying to make their way to where I stood in the open cargo doors. I just kept heaving plastic bottles of catsup as fast and as hard as I could heave.

The two men stopped when they heard the approaching sirens and put up their hands in a gesture of whoa-there-partner. My sides were heaving from all the bottle heaving. A Glen Safety Department cruiser barreled around the corner and into the back lot.

I turned wearily toward my best friend and her weak, struggling patient. I walked toward her, stepped on a catsup bottle, and fell against the blue tarp, smacking my face on the bottom of the truck floor.

Belinda screeched, *"Leslie!"*

I rolled onto my back, groaned, and then howled at a sudden pain in my arm. "Owwwww!"

Belinda was trying to help me to my feet when I was struck again in the arm. "Move, Les, the deer is waking up. He's kicking you."

I struggled to my feet with Belinda's help, all the time wailing, *"Owwww…my head…owwww…my arm!"*

Her arm around my shoulder, she helped me shuffle toward the open truck doors. I slid down her arm as if it was a rope and sat dangling my legs over the side.

Quinn Braddock and another officer were hopping around the puddles of catsup as they approached Sam and Scott. Belinda lowered herself to sit beside me in the doorway and again draped a comforting arm around my neck. I looked over at her and whispered in horror, "These creeps have been kidnapping and drugging our deer."

Tugging me closer to her side, she whispered, "I know, Les."

Sam said, "Hey, now look…"

I yelled in total freak-out mode, "You shut up. You just shut up… you… you… butcher!"

Sam shook his fist at me. "Well, of course, I'm a butcher!"

In her best Edith Bunker shriek, Belinda let him have it. *"Hey, buddy…my friend told you to shut up, so ZIP it!"*

Another patrol car came roaring around the side of the building with sirens blaring and lights flashing. Mark Edwards climbed out of the latest vehicle and switched places with Quinn Braddock, who had been talking with Sam the butcher.

Quinn walked toward where we sat in the truck's open doorway, scooped a panting Riff from the pavement, and plopped her into my arms. He asked, "What's the story this time, ladies?"

I started blubbering into Riff's fur, "They stole our deer. They… they…killed our deer and cut them up in…lit…little pieces. It's horrible. They killed Jane Doe. What are we going to tell Mrs. Towers?"

From somewhere Belinda produced a roll of paper towels, ripped off a sheet, and handed it to me. While I was busily blowing my nose, she filled Quinn in on events. "There is a deer in the back of this delivery truck. He…I believe it is a young buck…has been drugged but is starting to come around. I suggest some of your men lift it out of here before it wakes up. Otherwise, we're going to have one heck of a time getting it out of here."

Quinn leaned inside the truck as the blue tarp erupted every few seconds. "What the heck is a deer doing in the back of a catsup truck?"

Recovering my usually calm demeanor, I jammed the used paper towel into my pocket, and my knuckles bumped against the tranquilizer dart. I reached into my other pocket and pulled out my cell phone. "We've been trying to explain it to you, but it's complicated." I held out the cell phone to him. "Here, tell the 911 lady what's going on."

With feet in a wide stance and fisted hands on hips, he said, "But I don't know what is going on yet!"

I shook the phone at him. "Quinn, take the dang phone, get some of your men to lift this deer out of here, and we'll tell you all about it."

He snatched the phone and growled into the device, "Chief Braddock."

Mark Edwards and another officer abandoned Sam and Scott to come to the aid of the deer. I pointed at the prisoners. "Don't leave those two alone. They're the bad guys." Sam started stammering, and

Scott complained that the police had no right to be climbing all over his truck. Quinn cut off any further comment and ordered, "Mark, you and Matt put those two men in the back of a cruiser to be detained for questioning. Then come back here and retrieve this deer." He said a few more words into the phone, disconnected, and handed the phone back to me. I was careful to return the phone to the poison-dart-less pocket.

"Help us down from here, Quinn," Belinda said in her no-nonsense voice. He immediately lifted her to the pavement, then reached for me and Riff. We stood aside as Mark and Officer Matt vaulted into the back of the truck to struggle with the deer.

Belinda was impressive in her take-charge attitude. "Keep the tarp around it, boys, so it doesn't kick you."

She began to explain about the drugged deer in the delivery truck and how we had come to discover that Scott Epperling was poaching deer in the Glen. Meanwhile, I yanked off Tom's catsup smeared jacket and pitched it into the backseat of the Soul. We were interrupted by an officer calling, "Hey, Chief...come here. You need to see this!"

My arm ached, so I dropped Riff to the ground. She immediately took off again down the dirt track toward the officer standing in front of the prefab barn-like structure. The officer turned to walk behind the structure, Riff dancing at his feet.

Matt stayed behind with the dizzy deer. He was making soothing noises to it as we followed Quinn. A lot of men act tough, but they're really softies.

As we drew closer to the large outbuilding, I sniffed. "Ewwwww... they must have a thousand cats in there! What a stink!"

"Could be rabbits, Les; their urine stinks worse than a cat's."

Pinching my nostrils closed I honked, "Remember those two guys at the cornfield? They smelled bad like this."

As we were debating the source of the major stink, we rounded the building and stopped dead in our tracks and stared at a paddock behind the structure. Riff was racing up and down in front of the fence where at least a dozen deer were milling around. I caught her up in my arms, her little heart going a mile a minute, then handed her off to Belinda because my arm was still killing me.

We stood, Belinda looking over the top rail and me peering through a space between the rails. The deer were just noodling around, snacking on the grass. One of the deer limped over to us.

I yelled with delight, "It's Jane Doe! Belinda, we found Jane Doe!"

• • •

Things got very confusing for a while. We continued to tell our part of the story to Quinn, who shook his head from time to time. "Mrs. Barrett, you and Mrs. Honeycutt have got to stop these, for lack of a better word, quests of yours. You need to report these matters to my department."

I huffed indignantly. "We *did*. We filed a missing deer report. All you guys did was go poke around in the woods. Admit it. You had no intention of investigating whether our deer were getting poached."

"Shanghaied. The deer were shanghaied." Mark Edwards stood behind Quinn grinning at me.

I returned the grin, nodding, "Yes, shanghaied."

Quinn leaned on the fence. "We called the Wildlife Resource guys. They're on their way out. Not only that, but the TBI is sending Agent Donnelly."

I frowned. "Hailey? Why is the TBI involved in deer napping?"

"She's been in contact with us for some time now about Mr. Epperling and Mr. Tackett," he said evasively.

"What about Scott and Sam?"

"I'll let Agent Donnelly explain it to you later."

Chapter Eight

The Wildlife people showed up and took custody of the still-woozy deer from the truck. I couldn't help but notice that Matt refused to relinquish his hold on the animal totally. The Wildlife guy who seemed to be in charge, Dave Somebody, spent a lot of time talking with Sam and Scott back at the patrol car, then walked out to where we stood by the pen. We watched as Matt released our wobbly, rescued deer to mingle with the others in the pen.

Belinda called Dave over. "What do you think Scott used to drug the deer? I was thinking ketamine."

Dave nodded. "That would be my guess too, but we'll have to analyze what's left in that syringe. Where is it?"

I said, "I got hot and tossed my jacket into the backseat of my car. The poison dart is in one of the pockets. I'll get it for you in a bit." I pointed to a pile of dried corn and cornstalks, muttering under my breath to Belinda, "That stinky grandson of Sam's is involved in all this somehow. I just know it!"

Recognition lit her eyes. "Right. They were bringing the corn for the deer."

"Right...and he and that other guy stunk to high heaven."

Dave Somebody directed one of his men, "Might as well open the gate and let these deer go off into the woods."

"What? *No way is that happening!*" I hurried over and stood in front of the gate with arms crossed. Belinda joined me, with Riff tucked under one arm.

Dave explained, "There's no reason to leave them penned up. I've heard about deer being bred for hunting sport, but this setup is a new one on me. I got a partial confession from both men. Apparently this Scott fellow goes to the Glen at night and tranquilizes deer, then transports them out here to Tackett's place. That explains all the does they have, since it would be difficult to pick out a doe from a buck in the dark. When hunting season starts next week, they planned to sell hunting licenses to guys from out of state, let the deer loose in the woods, and guarantee at least one kill per crossbow hunter. If a doe was taken down, Sam would go ahead and butcher the meat for the hunter, and fail to report the kill. Pretty sweet plan those two had. I don't imagine the catsup people or the folks at the health department are going to be too thrilled about using a catsup truck to ferry sedated deer…but I'll let those agencies work out those charges. Now, there's no reason to keep these deer penned up any longer. We're going to let them go."

"Not out here you aren't." I raised my chin defiantly, and Belinda asserted, "I would say not."

Dave removed his hat and wiped an exasperated hand over his balding head. "And, why not? These woods are teeming with vegetation, and the creek is right there. The deer will do well out here. They'll stay in this area. The wild hogs will probably keep them from wandering into the Macoosa Wildlife Refuge. Those animals get pretty fierce. The deer will be smart enough to avoid that area."

"Hogs?" I yelped. "There are wild hogs around here? That crazy kind with the tusks and everything? I didn't know those things were rooting around in this area. They're vicious! There's no way you're letting Glen deer out around here. If the hunters don't get them, those tusky, snorting hogs will kill them for sure."

Belinda was shaking her head at Dave. "I really wish you hadn't mentioned the wild hogs, Dave."

"I just told you, ladies, those hogs are over in the game refuge and not around here. There are already a lot of deer in these woods though."

"If these woods are so great and crammed full of deer, why did Scott import Glen deer all the way out here?"

"Oh, there are deer out here all right…but the really sweet part of this scheme is the guarantee of a kill. Tackett has likely put the word out to some fellas in, say, Kentucky about how the northern portion of the county here is overrun with deer. As soon as the season starts, this area was fixin' to get real busy."

Catching on, I added scathingly, "And isn't it convenient that Sam Tackett's place just happens to set right here. Sam not only sells hunting permits, but he gets the additional bonus of being paid for his butchering services. You almost have to admire how well thought out their plan was."

I stood in front of Dave, looking up into his face. "You simply cannot release the deer into these woods. These deer"—I waved my hand at the penned animals—"are Fairlawn Glen deer. These are protected deer, *our* deer. They are not to be hunted. Heck, they've grown up in the Glen. Most of them are more like dogs than wild animals. No way are you leaving these deer out here in legal hunting grounds. And the game refuge isn't that far from here. I haven't forgotten about those crazed hogs."

"Ladies"—he gave an exasperated sigh—"we can't haul all these deer back to Fairlawn Glen."

Belinda stepped up and stared him down. "You most certainly can, and you will. Get a cattle truck or something."

Dave looked at Quinn for help. "Sorry, Dave, but I have to agree with the ladies. These animals don't know enough to be afraid of humans. It would be more slaughter than sport."

Dave swiped at his head and then resettled his hat. "Chief," he reasoned, "you and I both know there are deer out here on the north end that have naturally migrated out this way. Deer are skittish animals. A lot of them choose to move out this way just to get away from the Glen with all the people and residential development."

"*AHA!*" I ahaed.

"Aha, what?" Dave acknowledged my aha.

I jabbed a finger at him for emphasis, then waved my hand toward the woods. "Deer out here have *chosen* to move out this way."

"Ma'am, they're deer," he reasoned.

"Okay, let me give you a reasonable scenario as a comparison. Let's say I *choose* to move to Shanghai, Japan."

"China," Belinda corrected. "Shanghai is in China."

I waffled my hand. "Okay, okay, China. Say I *choose* to move to Shanghai, China. Since it was my idea to go there, I would simply have to learn to cope. Now let's say I'm walking around the kitchen of my townhome, eating an apple. Then some guy bursts in and shoots me full of knockout juice, and I wake up smack-dab in the middle of Shanghai. Is that fair? Is that the same thing? It wasn't *my idea* to move to Shanghai. I'm supposed to figure out all the Shanghai rules, laws, customs, and the language? I don't speak Chinese."

"Mrs. Barrett, I'm fairly certain Glen deer, and the deer out here on the north end, all speak deer."

I waffled my hand again. "Okay, forget about the language. The rest of the scenario works though. These Glen deer penned up out here didn't choose to be here. They didn't naturally migrate out this way for better berries or something."

Belinda laid a hand on Dave's shoulder. "Give it up, Dave. She's right."

He heaved a loud sigh. "Okay, I see your point, but our budget doesn't stretch that far. Somebody is going to have to cough up some funds."

"Talk to the TBI; evidently they have their noses stuck into all of this somehow," I suggested snidely.

"Why don't you ladies go on home and let Mrs. Towers know that her deer...um...Jane Doe is all right," Quinn suggested.

"We need to call Mrs. Towers. Jane is coming home with us."

"Excuse me?" Quinn frowned.

"Belinda, do you have your cell phone? Mine is in the pocket of my jacket."

She handed Riff off to me and dug deep into her pocket for her phone while I ordered, "Quinn, have one of your men run over to Mrs. Towers' and bring her out here."

"You have got to be kidding."

"No, not at all. Jane can ride back to the Glen with us. Mrs. Towers will be able to keep her calm during the ride."

"How are you planning to get the deer into your car?"

"Simple, we won't. We'll take her back in the catsup truck."

Quinn shook his head firmly. "I can't allow you to do that. That truck is evidence. Agent Donnelly told me specifically to hold the vehicle for her forensic people. She's not going to be too thrilled about all that spilled catsup as it is."

Belinda cut in, handing me her cell phone. "Scott Epperling has been taxiing deer from the Glen for quite some time in that truck. I don't much think one more is going to destroy any forensic evidence. You can have one of your officers drive the truck back to the Glen with Jane and Mrs. Towers, and then you can impound the truck and give it to whomever you choose. But that's how it's going to work. Now, Leslie is going to call Mrs. Towers. You get one of your officers to pick her up."

Quinn and Dave looked at one another helplessly and merely nodded in defeat. "Fine, go ahead, call Mrs. Towers. Good luck getting that deer in the truck, however."

I handed Riff off to Belinda and punched in Mrs. Towers' number.

Chapter Nine

Mrs. Towers was ecstatic. "Leslie, thank you! Oh my goodness, I have been *so* worried about Jane!"

"She looks okay, Mrs. Towers, but we have to get her back to your place. One of Quinn's guys is on his way to pick you up. I don't think we can get her into the truck without your help."

"I'll get a little bag of produce to bring along. Oh, John is going to be so happy to have her back!"

I disconnected with a broad grin for Belinda and tucked the cell phone into her pocket.

"Let me guess," she deadpanned, "she's giving you, *the great detective*, all the credit."

We broke out into goofy, girly giggles. Poor Riff was about to drop from all the excitement, so Belinda carried her to the car, and I commandeered a bottle of water from one of the officers. The two of us leaned against the Soul and watched Riff happily slop water all over the ground.

"She's a brave little thing, Leslie," my best friend observed.

I bumped her shoulder affectionately. "Yeah, she's my second best friend in the entire world. I wonder what Hailey Donnelly has to do with all this? The TBI don't usually pursue animal rustlers, as far as I know."

We were still discussing the subject when Quinn's officer arrived with Mrs. Towers. He pulled up beside my Soul, and we went to greet her.

Through the now-open passenger-side door, she gushed, "Thank you, girls… oh my goodness, thank you. My walker is in the back there."

"It's a heck of a walk to where these men have been holding Jane." I leaned down to see the driver and recognized Officer Edwards. "Mark, could you possibly drive her back there to the pen, please."

"Sure," he grinned. "My pleasure. I don't get many calls that are this much fun!"

Belinda slammed the door, one-handed Riff, and we trotted behind the cruiser.

"You need to let me have a look at your face and arm, Les. Your face is already a little bit swollen. I'll get some ice from Tackett's place for you." That's Belinda, always the concerned nurse.

Jogging behind the cruiser, we once again encountered the major stink of the outbuilding. "Rabbits! These jerks are breeding rabbits! They probably release three hundred rabbits at rabbit season!"

Mrs. Towers had the passenger-side door open, and one of the Wildlife guys was assisting her from the vehicle while another hauled out the walker.

I pointed at the gimpy deer. "That is Jane, isn't it?"

"Oh, Jane, baby," she burbled tearfully, smacking a plastic bag of produce into my chest while she stumped past me on her way to the fence. It was touching to watch. Mrs. Towers peered between the fence slats (she is short, like me) and dangled her arm in the opening. "Come here, baby. I've been so worried about you."

It didn't take Jane long to recognize her benefactor, and soon she was snuffling her muzzle in Mrs. Towers' outstretched hand. "Leslie, give me something from the bag," she ordered.

I fished out some lettuce, and we watched as Jane nibbled lettuce while the other less-domesticated deer looked on jealously. Belinda and I had tears leaking from our eyes, and I heard more than one rumble of a man's throat clearing; not the least of them was Quinn's.

Recovering his composure, he gruffly called out, "Mark, drive that delivery truck back here, will you? I'm assuming we have the keys."

"Yes, sir, we do, sir." Mark pulled the keys from his pocket and jogged up the dirt track to collect the truck.

Remembering about the rabbits, I hollered, "Hey, Quinn, when is rabbit hunting season?"

He frowned and shrugged at Dave. "Is there such a thing as rabbit hunting season, Dave?"

"It starts November eighth. Why?"

Quinn swiveled his head my way. "Why?"

I waved my arm at the outbuilding. "Because I suspect these guys were breeding rabbits for hunting season in that big, stinky building. Either that or they have teensy weensy dart guns full of bunny knockout juice. Belinda and I ran across one of Sam Tackett's grandsons and a buddy of his at a corn maze down the road. They smelled just like this place."

"Don't concern yourself with that building, ladies," Quinn ordered firmly.

"Don't tell me you guys can't smell that ammonia! That's either a rabbit farm or a cathouse!" I insisted.

Several of the men chuckled, and Mark Edwards choked on a laugh. "Cathouse! That's rich." Another man called out, "Hey, maybe it's a chicken ranch!"

They all laughed at that.

I mumbled an aside to Belinda, "Quinn knows something about that building." She nodded in agreement.

• • •

While the men milled around figuring out how to get Jane into the delivery truck and round up a trailer for the rest of the deer, I slipped away to get a better look at the stinky building. The closer I got, the worse the odor. I scurried around the building and found a side door. It was unlocked. I opened the door a crack to peer inside, pinching my nostrils closed at the stench.

A large hand slapped the door shut with a thud. I whirled around, gasping from the surprise, and the smell.

One hand on my nose and one at my throat, I honked, "Quinn, don't sneak up on a person like that."

"What are you doing, Mrs. Barrett?"

I released my nose and narrowed my eyes, wiping away ammonia-induced tears. "What's been going on in there? Belinda thinks the place is full of rabbits. If there are rabbits penned up in the middle of their own stink, we have to get them out."

"It isn't rabbits, Leslie."

"Well, chickens then. It's inhumane to leave any living animals in that stench!"

Taking my arm, he led me away from the building. "There are no animals in that building, Leslie. Trust me."

"But…that *smell!*"

"I know. It's awful. Agent Donnelly will explain everything."

"Hailey? What on earth does Hailey have to do with a building full of whatever's causing that stench?"

• • •

It didn't take much coaxing to get Jane into the truck. She limped through the gate with Mrs. Towers' hand caressing her neck. The other deer tried to follow, and Dave (the Wildlife guy) shooed them back. "Wait your turn. We're getting a truck for the rest of you."

I put a grateful hand on his arm. "Thank you, Dave. Somehow we will see that you get reimbursed for the expense."

"I wouldn't worry about it too much, Mrs. Barrett." He grinned down at me.

While the guys held the truck's back doors open, Mrs. Towers ordered, "Somebody help me into this thing. Good heavens, what happened here? Is this blood? It looks like a massacre!"

"It's just catsup," I called to her.

Once established, she clucked, "Well, that's a relief." Little Jane Doe was already craning her neck toward Mrs. Towers as she ordered, "Couple of you men hand her up to me. Don't you worry now; she's as docile as a little lamb."

Dave scooped the small doe into his arms and lifted her into the truck.

Belinda instructed, "Mrs. Towers, lead her over to that blue tarp," then she barked, "Somebody get a blanket for her to sit on." Everybody went scrambling, except me.

Once they were both comfortable, the doors were swung shut. Quinn ordered, "Mark, you drive the truck; I'll follow you in the cruiser. Once Mrs. Towers and Jane are home, we'll take the truck to the Safety Department, and Agent Donnelly can collect it there."

We had a minicaravan all the way down Trendle Road. We followed the cruiser. Belinda was still driving since the cockpit was already all cranked out for her tall frame. On the way she told me about the drug, ketamine. "It's used in human and veterinary medicine as a general anesthetic. We occasionally used it in the ER as a painkiller, particularly with patients with compromised respirations...like asthma. Nowadays it's commonly used by oral surgeons. I believe it started out as a horse tranquilizer, but I could be mistaken about that."

"Those jerks, using something like that on deer. Horses are a lot bigger than deer."

"Actually, I believe the lingering side effects make one pleasantly goofy."

I took the opportunity to relate my conversation with Quinn about the stinky building. "It sounds as though we have stumbled onto something Hailey Donnelly is in the middle of again. Quinn swears there are no rabbits or chickens in that building."

"I don't know what other animals smell like that…bats, maybe?"

"Bats?" I shook my head. "That makes no sense whatsoever. Nobody hunts bats. Besides, Quinn said there were no animals at all in that building."

"Well, that rules out chicken hunting too."

***

W e thanked the two men profusely once they lifted Mrs. Towers and Jane from the truck.

Mrs. Towers was already making her way across the grass, with Jane hobbling behind like a puppy.

Quinn looked at the two of them and smiled. "They're quite a pair, aren't they?" Then he cleared his throat and said, "Mrs. Barrett, Mrs. Honeycutt, I'll call you after I've spoken with Agent Donnelly. We should probably meet at my office sometime tomorrow."

"Not too early," I pleaded. "Hey, what's the TBI's interest in Scott Epperling and Sam Tackett?"

"Tomorrow, Mrs. Barrett. I'll call you with the time."

We followed Mrs. Towers and Jane. Riff hung over my arm like a fox fur. The poor baby was exhausted. Belinda carried the sack of produce. Catching sight of us, Mrs. Towers waved her arm, ordering, "Belinda, empty that sack onto the grass just beyond the patio, please. We'll go inside and watch. I'm hoping John Doe will show up."

She did as ordered, then sat with us at the kitchen table to watch through the sliding patio doors.

"Mrs. Towers, do you have any of Riff's wet food?" She always keeps a couple of cans around for Riff just in case.

"Sure, you know where they are. Get down a couple of shallow cereal bowls for her."

Soon Riff's face was buried in the puddle of wet dog food. Mrs. Towers also keeps Diet Coke for Belinda and me, so I snatched three of them from the refrigerator.

I downed half the bottle, wincing as the cold liquid passed my scraped lips. Noticing (not much gets past Mrs. Towers), she instructed Belinda, "Get one of those plastic zipper bags and put some ice in it for Leslie. Poor little thing is all banged up."

Belinda hopped to. "Leslie, I'm sorry. I forgot about the ice." In minutes I had my banged-up arm resting on one bag of ice while I held another to the side of my face. Finally full, Riff staggered over and collapsed on my foot, her face still covered with mashed-up dog food. I mumbled into the ice, "I'm not picking you up, Whiff. You're a meth."

Again, Belinda hopped to and scrubbed Riff's face with a wet paper towel, depositing her on my lap when she was presentable.

"Fanks," I mumbled into the ice.

I love this woman.

"Flook!" I burbled into the ice, and pointed with my good hand. We watched as John stepped from the copse of trees. He approached Jane slowly at first, then practically galloped across the grass. The two deer companions nuzzled each other; then John dipped his head to partake of what produce was left.

All three of us sat at the kitchen table blubbering like idiots into paper towels.

Chapter Ten

I was a mess. I had a big, blood-crusted knot on my face where I'd slammed it on the floor of the delivery truck. I had bruises on my arm where the terrified deer had struck me while flailing around inside the tarp.

I left Belinda in my kitchen scooping more ice for my wounds. Carrying Tom's catsup smeared jacket, I walked wearily through my bedroom toward the bathroom. My face and arm throbbing, I stuck my hand into the pocket of Tom's jacket, planning to throw the bloody/ snotty paper towel into the bathroom wastebasket. Something sharp bit my hand, and I yanked it from the pocket. At first I thought I had stabbed myself with my fingernail. To my dismay, the business end of the traquilizer dart was embedded in the palm of my hand.

Oh God, what do I do? I probably need to do…some…thing. What was it I was supposed to do?

I yanked the dart from my hand, staggered toward the bed, and passed out.

I came to lying facedown on the bed, drooling onto the comforter. Riff was licking my face, which I hate. She smelled like catsup. "Sop it, Miff," I mumbled.

What happened to me?

My head couldn't think. My head hurt.

I've been stabbed!

I stared back and forth between my hand and the syringe on the comforter. I tried to stand, but wobbled and sank to the floor. I couldn't figure out what it was I was supposed to be doing.

I could hear Belinda bumping around in the kitchen. *"Blenna!"* I yelled in a half sob. She appeared at my bedroom door clutching two bags full of ice.

Rushing to my side, she dumped the bags on the bed and knelt beside it. "What happened?"

"I'm stabbed…my hand…sommmm ath-hole stabbed me." I flapped my hand in front of her face as proof. Her eyes flicked from mine to the comforter on the bed and widened when she saw the dart lying there.

Riff was sniffing the dart, and Belinda yelped, "Riff, get away from that."

Riff jumped at the tone of her voice, and I wailed, *"Donnn't ya yell a Riff!"* Then I sniffled and noticed the color of the blouse she was wearing. It was the most beautiful color I had ever seen. "Ooooooo… Blenna, you are beautiful; you look jus like a yallow finch. I like yellow finches. I ever tell you 'bout the yellow finches?"

"Stay still. I'm calling 911." She reached for my bedside phone.

"Nooooo…you sick, Blenna?" I wailed. "Donnn't die, Blenna… donnn't wan Blenna die." I wept at the thought of losing the best friend I had in the entire world. It wasn't fair. First Tom and now Belinda.

She knelt on the floor beside me. "Nobody is dying, Les. You stuck yourself with the syringe. You dosed yourself with some ketamine. It'll wear off, honey; you're going to be fine."

"Katmiiine! Superman lergic to katmiiine! We will die! Haff to save us."

Loud sirens were suddenly everywhere. I flung myself backward. "Whas that! My God…whas that? Air raid! Blenna, get down. Iss an air raid!"

"It's the ambulance, honey."

Filled to the brim with grief, I began to weep. "Amlance? Oh no, Blennaa sick. Amlance taking Blenna awayyy."

A bit of commotion distracted me, and I looked up into the face of a nice-looking young man. "Hi," I quipped. "Who are you?"

By the time I arrived at the emergency room, my brain was beginning to clear from the effects of the minor dose of ketamine. I was given some oxygen, which made me cough; but they gave me more oxygen, and then some water. My face and arm thoroughly doctored, they checked me all over. Thankfully Belinda had grabbed another jacket from my closet so we could throw away Tom's catsup stained one (good-bye, Tom's jacket). The doctor and nurses freaked out when they first saw me. I looked like a bloodied madwoman, which I was in a way. They released me with instructions to drink plenty of water and watch for signs of concussion such as nausea and confusion.

I thought that was rich: watch for signs of confusion after I had just gone through my one-and-only acid trip. What a hoot.

Chapter Eleven

Belinda called me at 9:30 the next morning to tell me that we had to be at Quinn's office at 11:00.

I whined, "Don't you want to know how I'm feeling this morning? I mean, I did get beat up and toxically compromised yesterday."

"Okay, how are you feeling this morning?"

"Sore and grumpy. How about you?"

"Sore and grumpy," she admitted. "I can't wait to find out what charges they filed against Scott and Sam. It makes my blood boil just thinking about those poor deer."

"I can't wait to find out what Agent Hailey Donnelly has to do with all this."

I went into the bathroom and stared at my reflection. I looked like one of those starving little kids they show on TV. I had a bandage plastered over the cut next to the lump on my forehead. Fortunately, the cut had not required stitches. My forehead was the color of an eggplant. I was getting one hell of a shiner too. I grinned and congratulated myself on my war wounds. I also had two sore, bruised areas on my right arm where the Bambi from hell had kicked me.

We breezed into the meeting looking our best. It had taken a lot of effort, and makeup, to cover this girl. Chief Quinn, Mark Edwards, and Dave-the-Wildlife-guy stood as we entered. Belinda had Riff.

After everybody commented on my face and Belinda recounted our hospital run of the night before, we finally got down to business.

Dave asked, "So, it was ketamine in that dart?"

"Yes" Belinda nodded. "A pretty strong concentration too. Huh, Leslie?"

I laughed. "Oh yeah. It was like being on a Tilt-A-Whirl!"

Quinn read a summary of the charges against Scott Epperling and Sam Tackett. The Wildlife Resources people were slapping Scott with a boatload of fines and jurisdictional misdemeanors. Quinn was also charging Scott with trespassing for tramping around on Glen properties on his narcoleptic missions.

On behalf of the Wildlife Resource people, Dave jumped in. "Epperling is being charged with spotlighting deer."

"Spotlighting? What's that?" I asked.

"It's a cowardly form of hunting wild animals at night. A hunter tries to locate a deer in the woods, usually by sound, or in Scott's case, they scout the area beforehand and identify the paths the deer use. Once they locate a deer, the hunter shines a bright light at the deer. Temporarily blinded, the deer freezes in place."

"Like a deer in headlights. I know just how they feel," I confessed. "The night I tried to look through the window into Scott's garage, the light from my reading glasses bounced right back at me, and I almost fried my eyeballs! It took several minutes to recover well enough to make it back across the street."

Dave stared at me curiously and shook his head. "Don't tell me. I don't want to know; anyway, while the deer was momentarily blind, Epperling shot it with a tranquilizer gun. It looks more like a sniper rifle than a handgun."

Belinda and I stared at each other in comprehension. "*Thwip thwip*," we said in unison.

"What's that?" Dave asked.

"The sound we heard in the woods…it sounded like *thwip thwip*."

Dave nodded. "Yeah, it's a puny sound coming from such a lethal-looking weapon."

When it appeared that he was finished, I asked incredulously, "That's it? Trespassing, farm animal violations, flashing deer...what about poaching! Scott Epperling shanghaied our deer! He drugged them and then penned them up. He and Sam Tackett planned to have them murdered, but we got to them before they could carry out their plan. Glen deer are helpless. The stupid animals don't know enough to be afraid of humans! Not only that but what about me? I'm all beat up because of those two men. Charge them both with assault or something."

Belinda jumped into the fray fighting mad. "Yeah, what about Leslie's injuries? Who knows, she could have died from that needle stick!"

"Yeah!" I pumped my fist. "Ow."

Quinn sighed. "Mrs. Barrett, you told us you tripped over catsup bottles... bottles that, you were lobbing at Epperling and Tackett. They want to press assault charges against you! And you stuck yourself with that dart. You were supposed to turn it over to Dave."

On my feet now, I yelled, "I fell over a body! A body that had no business being in the back of a catsup truck!"

Dave frowned. "What body?"

Quinn answered him with a curt "She means the deer, Dave."

"But the deer wasn't dead."

"That is hardly the point, Dave," I said in a more reasonable tone of voice.

Sheesh, I am surrounded by morons.

Quinn was sounding tired. "The Department of Public Health is investigating, and there will be fines there as well. The owners and distributors of Papa Field's Catsup are being fined, as well as Scott Epperling."

"Well, that makes all the difference in the world!" I sat down with a harrumph. "I am never buying Field's Catsup again. In fact, I just may boycott all catsup...and ketchup as well." I frowned. "By the way, what's the difference between catsup and ketchup? I've always wondered. And, how come there isn't another way to spell *mustard?*"

Nobody knew, but the question threw Quinn off stride.

Belinda took advantage of my misdirection by asking, "What about Sam Tackett? I don't doubt that he is a legitimate butcher of game animals—just like his sign says—but he was running an illegal operation out there!"

Dave answered, "Yes, he has also received some hefty fines for keeping game animals on his property. If those animals had been ponies, he would still have been over the legal limit per acreage."

"People don't shoot ponies." I aimed a steely eyed glare at Dave. "I'm not aware of an open hunting season on ponies, Dave."

Dave squirmed. "No, ma'am, that is true. However, once released into those woods, if a legally registered hunter had killed one of those animals during the legally designated hunting period, the hunter would not have committed a crime."

"He would if he was deliberately shooting a doe," I insisted. "This isn't right. Sam Tackett is getting off way too easily."

Quinn summarized, "In summary, both men are appropriately fined and punished." He dismissed Dave courteously. "Dave, thank you for coming in for the meeting. We appreciate it."

Dave resisted the invitation to leave. "Before I leave I need to mention something here. I know how tempting it is to feed deer, especially one with a bad leg, but it isn't a good idea to get the animals dependent on humans for their food. Mrs. Towers means well, but one of these days she is liable to open her patio door and find a black bear sitting there waiting for breakfast."

Belinda's *ahem* interrupted the lesson. "Dave, we try to avoid the subject of bears. Leslie is especially sensitive to the subject."

"What I wanted to tell you ladies is this: Mrs. Towers' deer...um, Jane Doe...is a young doe. I suspect she's less than a year old. When I lifted her into the truck, I took a look at her leg. It appears to me as though it had been broken and, when left untreated, mended badly. Because she is such a young animal, the break is fairly recent...perhaps even during the birthing process. I contacted one of the vets who work with us on game animals, and she is willing to examine Jane."

I leaned toward Dave. "What can she do for her?"

"We won't know until she sees her; potentially the leg could be rebroken and set correctly. Hopefully, she'll be capable of fending for herself once it mends."

"What about John?"

"Who?"

"John, Jane's friend, John Doe. John is pathetic without Jane." I glanced at Belinda, who was nodding in agreement.

"Are they pretty close to the same size?"

We both nodded at Dave.

"Male and female deer don't buddy up unless it's rutting season...or a Walt Disney movie. Deer don't have conversations with rabbits and skunks either."

I frowned. "What are you talking about?"

Belinda sighed. "*Bambi*, Leslie. He's talking about the movie."

"Oh yeah. Thumper and Flower." I glowered at Dave. "What's wrong with Thumper and Flower. I liked that part of the movie. The ending sucked big-time. Poor little Bambi running around through the smoke crying, 'Mama...Mama.'" I shook my head. "That Walt Disney must have had an awful childhood. And don't even get me started on *Old Yeller*."

Belinda interrupted my movie critique. "Give it a rest, Leslie. We get the point."

Dave cleared his throat. "It's possible that they are twins. It's not unusual."

"Now that you mention it, they do look a lot alike. Except for John's junk, I mean."

Belinda snorted. "All deer look alike, Les. It isn't like you can pick one out of a lineup or anything." Then in a bad imitation of me she pointed into the air. "It was that one right there, Officer. That's the deer that attacked my car without provocation."

"Shutup, Belinda." I looked at Dave. "What about the vet costs?"

"Y'all can discuss that with the vet, Dr. Norris, Dr. Wanda Norris." Leaning in my direction, he handed me a business card. "She said she'd be happy to take a look at Jane. Dr. Norris does some pro bono work for us. She would have to make that determination, however. The deer would be looking at some rehabilitation time as well. Give Wanda a call."

Quinn followed Dave to the door and, leaning into the lobby, said, "Agent Donnelly, will you come in now, please?"

"Oh shoot. I meant to ask Dave whether wild turkeys can fly."

"Turkeys can't fly, Les."

"But…"

TBI Agent Hailey Donnelly huffed brusquely into the room. Belinda and I had become acquainted with Hailey over the summer. She is thirty-something, fit, dark blond, and she started yelling the moment she entered the room. "Mrs. Barrett, Mrs. Honeycutt, you could have jeopardized…" She stopped midsentence, and her jaw dropped. "Leslie, just look at your face. Are you all right?"

It was a sweet moment. Hailey likes to talk tough, but we sort of bonded during some harrowing moments last summer. "Yes, honey,

I'm all right. Belinda and I had a bit of a raucous afternoon yesterday. What's your involvement in all this?"

It turned out that the TBI had been watching both Scott Epperling and Sam Tackett. They had been the subjects of scrutiny by the TBI for the distribution of methamphetamine. Sam's grandsons made the crap in that prefab barn-like structure, and Sam and Scott moved the drugs via the catsup truck.

"That methomphomen stuff...I've heard of that. Isn't that like rat poison? Why would anyone intentionally take rat poison unless they were trying to commit suicide, and I would imagine there are easier ways to commit suicide then taking rat poison."

"It's called methamphetamine," Belinda clarified, "commonly referred to as meth."

"Yeah, meth. The kids make it out of cough medicine or something; I know about that. I can't get Sudafed anymore over the counter unless I show them my driver's license, birth certificate, and a note from my mother. What a pain in the butt that is. Makes me feel like a criminal." A horrible realization hit me. "Do you mean to tell me that while Scott was hauling drugged Glen deer out to Sam's place, the poor deer were exposed to that methomtrampoline stuff in his delivery truck?"

Hailey tilted her head and narrowed her eyes. "What ...?"

Belinda's eyes sparked with an epiphany. "Les, that explains the elaborate security setup with the cameras and motion sensors, and that ammonia smell. It isn't a barn full of bunnies, cats, chickens, or bats. They were making methamphetamine in that metal building!" She turned to Hailey with a grimace. "That place stank to high heaven. I'm surprised it took the authorities this long to investigate! Not only that, but Leslie and I encountered Sam Tackett's grandson and a buddy of his loading up dried ears of corn over at the corn maze on Trendle. That smell followed them around like Pigpen's dust cloud from "Peanuts."

How could somebody not have recognized that smell for what it was?"

I had my own epiphany. "The freezer! Belinda, I'll bet Sam Tackett had the drugs stored in that freezer in those catsup boxes! I knew that a catsup-related hoarding disorder sounded goofy!" I leaned toward Hailey. "He had those drugs in the freezer, didn't he?"

Hailey was googly-eyed. "You were in the walk-in freezer?"

"I was just looking around."

Belinda interrupted with a haughty sniff. "I told her it was foolish and dangerous, but she never listens to me."

"You weren't anywhere near me when I went into that freezer, Belinda. You were waltzing around with the bodies in the back of the slaughterhouse."

"Oh yeah, I forgot."

Hailey looked back and forth at the two of us, shaking her head. "I won't even ask you to explain those comments. To answer your question about the freezer, Mrs. Barrett, yes, the boys were manufacturing crystal meth and cutting it into salable chunks."

"That's what I saw in those little plastic bags!" I whooped triumphantly. "Does it look like ice?"

"Yes, it's often referred to as ice or hot ice on the street."

I frowned. "What do they do, swallow chunks of that crap?"

Belinda leaned toward me. "I'll explain it to you later, Les."

My eyes widened. "You know how to administer hot ice?"

"Later, Les." Belinda turned toward Hailey and demanded angrily, "What took you people so long to bring charges against these men?" Ever the lawyer's wife, she narrowed her eyes. "Do you have enough evidence to bring charges against all these men?"

"Mrs. Honeycutt," Hailey complained, "I just told you. We have been investigating the site for weeks."

"Not very well, obviously. If Leslie was able to stumble across their narcotic freezer stash, surely your guys could have gotten a search warrant and discovered it a long time ago."

I mumbled, "Well, it wasn't like I was staggering around in there or anything."

Hailey straightened in her seat. "As a matter of fact, Mrs. Honeycutt, we did get a search warrant last evening, and we were able to take down the entire operation. Scott Epperling is being charged with transporting and selling crystal meth, mostly around Knoxville. Sam Tackett and both grandsons are being charged with the manufacturing, storing, and distribution of meth. Crystal meth is frequently stored in freezers to lock out moisture that can potentially damage the product. Not only that, but we have reviewed the security footage from the parking lot."

Uh-oh.

She glared at Belinda. "Mrs. Honeycutt, your vehicle was seen skulking around the parking lot at Tackett's the night before the raid. Your license place was picked up on the security camera."

My friend reeled back and huffed in her best Belinda-huffing voice, "We were not skulking. We were merely turning around in Mr. Tackett's parking lot. I don't believe that is against the law."

"Don't deny it. The two of you were up to no good out there, in the dead of night. Security cameras picked you up again careening around the other side of the building to make a hasty getaway."

"Doesn't Mr. Tackett have security cameras in the back of his place?" I inquired as innocently as I could manage.

She narrowed her eyes. "No."

"That's not being very thorough on Mr. Tackett's part. Anyway, like Belinda said, we were just turning around to head back to the Glen." Having dismissed Hailey's questions as unimportant, I whispered, "Belinda, how do they take that meth stuff?"

"Later, Leslie."

"Well, fine," I sniffed at my friend, and asked Hailey, "What was the purpose of the elaborate security system inside the building? We just happened to notice it when we were out there visiting the place the other day. The day we discovered the never-ending train of Papa Field's Catsup."

Quinn must have been feeling left out, because he interjected, "Sam's place was getting a reputation in the meth community. He was concerned about break-ins, both because of the drugs and the large amounts of cash he kept in his office safe."

I looked at Quinn. "With all that security, it was pretty stupid not to have a lock on that freezer."

Quinn nodded with a tiny twinkle in his eye. "Yes, that was careless. Obviously he wasn't aware of the reputation you and Mrs. Honeycutt have carved out for yourselves."

Belinda and I shared a grin.

"Chief, that is hardly the point here."

I snapped at the agent, "Okay, Hailey, what is the point? My head hurts."

"Your interference yesterday could have jeopardized months of hard investigative work! You both need to stop interfering in matters better left to the authorities. And skulking around out there at night was just plain stupid."

I was rendered speechless by her condescending attitude. Belinda all but yelled at her, "We were *not* skulking. Boy, that's gratitude for you. Leslie and I stopped a regular crime spree last summer with no help at all from you! You never even showed up, even after Leslie called you to request backup." Belinda's indignant fury was beautiful to behold.

Hailey stammered, "I-I-I got a message. All I got was a message about the two of you and a cemetery."

"And where are Scott Epperling, Sam Tackett, and Sam's two

grandsons now? And that other boy, the one who was with Tackett's grandson at the corn maze?" I demanded in my haughtiest voice.

"What was his name?" Hailey asked.

Quinn interjected, "They are in the county jail awaiting charges, including the Thicke boy."

Recovering her autocratic tone, Hailey lectured, "Ladies, you interfered with a TBI operation that has been in the works for weeks."

"Belinda already asked you why these men weren't arrested until now. What the heck have you-all been waiting for?"

"We were building the case. Taking down an operation like this cannot be done in a slapdash fashion!"

"In other words…you were waiting for proof."

"We were building the case."

"And now you have proof?"

"Well, yes. The meth lab was set up in that outbuilding. Our forensic guys are combing the delivery truck and have already discovered significant traces of methamphetamine, not to mention the contents of that freezer and the stacks of cash in the safe."

"And traces of shanghaied deer?"

Massaging her temples, Hailey gritted her teeth. "Mrs. Barrett, what I am trying to get through to the two of you is that, because of your interference, you jeopardized the success of our operation, *and* you could have been seriously injured!"

I stabbed a finger at my face, and in a vernacular I picked up from my granddaughter and can't seem to shake, "*Hell-lo?* I *was* injured. These pretty colors on my face are not courtesy of Mary Kay Cosmetics! Did you even know that I wound up in the ER last night gathering yet more proof that those men were drugging our deer?"

Her jaw went slack. "Wha…?"

I flapped my arms. "I've had enough of your thin skin, Hailey. The truth is, because of our efforts yesterday, four criminals are off the street, a hot ice racket has been busted, and the Glen deer are back home in protected territory. Isn't that about it?" I turned to my best friend in the entire world. "Belinda, I don't know about you, but I'm tired of all this. My head hurts. I'm leaving now. Are you coming?"

"I certainly am, Leslie," she huffed, and we stood in preparation to exit.

Quinn called after us, "Wait a minute, ladies, we're not finished here. This meeting has gotten way out of hand."

With my nose in the air I advised Chief Quinn Braddock, "You can sit here and kick this around all day if you want to, but we have better things to do. We need to report to Mrs. Towers."

Before leaving the room, I lobbed a parting shot at Hailey. "Agent Donnelly, you are never going to last with the TBI if you don't get a handle on your petty jealousy."

Hailey was verbally beating her chest as we headed for the exit. "They could have totally blown several weeks of work right out of the water. Those are two of the most infuriating women I have ever met."

Quinn's rumbling voice followed us out the door along with Mark Edwards' snorting laughter.

When Belinda opened the door, I blurted, "Wait a minute, I forgot something." I hurried back to the office door, gave two knuckle raps, opened the door, and stuck my head inside. Everybody turned to look at me, but my eyes were focused only on Hailey. "There's a *call girl* who goes by the name of Kiki. She has been missing for several days. Kiki hung around in the parking lot next to the furniture store on East Street with the rest of the hookers, um, I mean call girls. According to my source, Kiki is in her late teens or early twenties, skinny, with badly dyed blond hair. You might want to check into her disappearance. Belinda and I doubt there's any connection between Scott Epperling and Sam Tackett's *hot ice slash deer-smuggling operation*, but you might want to look into it. The parking lot is across the street from Papa Field's Catsup. I don't believe in coincidences. Bye."

I hustled back to Belinda. "I suggested Hailey look into Kiki's disappearance. Now, explain to me how people swallow those big chunks of hot ice."

"I said I'd tell you later."

"It's later."

Epilogue

One Month Later

I was almost disappointed that I didn't have any psychedelic flashbacks from my ketamine trip.

Belinda and I waited to see whether we'd be subpoenaed as witnesses in the Scott Epperling–Sam Tackett mess. No such luck. Fairlawn Glen catsup smeared deer would never have the satisfaction or closure of looking their captors in the eye. Everything was being taken care of behind the scenes with lawyers and judges, some nonsense about penal codes.

Dr. Wanda Norris agreed to take Jane Doe on as a patient. According to the doctor, Jane had sustained a fracture between the knee and hip of her front leg as a very young fawn. The leg had healed at a wonky angle, causing Jane to walk like Walter Brennan on the *Real McCoys*. She didn't advise surgery and splinting since Jane didn't appear to be in pain and had adapted her gait to allow for the disability. She didn't like Jane's odds of survival in the wild—even within our protected community. Being hit by a car was a very real possibility. When startled, a healthy deer can practically fly from the path of a vehicle. Jane's impairment would cut her chances of escape significantly. Jane is in the safe hands of Dr. Norris until the doctor finds a suitable home for her at one of the petting zoos around Knoxville.

John and Jane will move together to the safety of a petting zoo. The two may very well be siblings, but nobody is curious enough to fund genetic testing. Dave insists that boy and girl deer don't form plutonic relationships, nor do they respect familial taboos when it comes to procreation. He's wrong, of course. Belinda, Mrs. Towers, and I have pledged one hundred dollars apiece to cover Jane's medical costs. The men and women at the Glen Safety Department and the Wildlife Resource people are also taking donations to cover the continued care and feeding of the two once a zoo can be located.

Lilly did some amateur sleuthing of her own and discovered that Kiki is actually twenty-year-old Nora June Mayberry. Nora June had been saving her earnings so she could return to her training as a dental hygienist. Good for Nora June. I admire a girl who knows what she wants and puts in the hard work to get it.

I didn't call Agent Hailey Donnelly with an update on Kiki, the missing call girl. Let Hailey do some investigating for a change. Heck, Belinda and I shouldn't have to do everything.

Hello Readers,

I can't see or hear you but if you're reading this, then you've just read my book, *Shanghaied.*

Thanks for allowing Leslie & Belinda to inhabit your brain for a bit. They run around in mine like a couple of caffeinated hamsters.

A brief review of your reading experience on Amazon, Goodreads, or another review site that I haven't discovered yet would be greatly appreciated. I want my publisher to keep signing up my books, but I need something to point to when I say "Well, someone liked them!" And be sure and check out the first book in the Leslie and Belinda series, *Daredevil.*

Follow me on Facebook, and check out my website to keep track of what I'm up to. By the way, it seems that Leslie & Belinda have already caught the scent of another mystery in the Glen and I can't wait to release the hamsters!

~ *Linda*

Follow me on:
Facebook: Linda S. Browning
Twitter: @LindaSBrowning
Website: lindabrowning.net

Made in the USA
Middletown, DE
18 March 2021